Intoxicating Agent

By

Joyce Dudley

Many of the quotations used at the beginning of each chapter were adapted from Black's Law Dictionary, by Henry Campbell Black, M.A. West Publishing Company.

Cover design by Jim Kreyger and Chris Master.
Cover photo by Jim Kreyger.
Photo of author by Denise Retallack.

ISBN 0-7414-2977-2

Published by:
INFINITY
PUBLISHING.COM
1094 New DeHaven Street, Suite 100
West Conshohocken, PA 19428-2713
Info@buybooksontheweb.com
www.buybooksontheweb.com
Toll-free (877) BUY BOOK
Local Phone (610) 941-9999
Fax (610) 941-9959

Printed in the United States of America
Printed on Recycled Paper
Published January 2006

DEDICATION

To all the intoxicating Agents…
I've had the pleasure of working with.

Acknowledgments

Daily I wake up, pre-dawn, in the same town as my loving family: Norma, John, Sam, Chris, Matt, Mike, and our pups Moose and Emmitt - for this I am eternally grateful.

Weekdays I am surrounded by caring, smart people in the Santa Barbara County District Attorney's Office and in our courts – for this I am deeply appreciative.

Several times a week, crime victims walk into my office and describe the worst moment of their life, seeking only justice in return. I am in awe of these victims/survivors and feel privileged to be a part of their healing process. My characters were created to honor their bravery. I hope in writing this novel I can give their pain and courage a voice.

I don't believe any one can write a trustworthy novel without the help and support of friends and colleagues who are willing to read and criticize their work. Reading a book, as it emerges, is an arduous process. Heartfelt thanks to the following consultants, editors, and readers: Joe Poire, Santa Barbara City Fire Department, Dr. Robert Anthony, Santa Barbara County Coroner/Pathologist, Ed Stetson, Santa Barbara Harbor Patrol, Carol Mosely, Director Rape Prevention Program, U.C.S.B., Elsa Granados, Santa Barbara Rape Crisis Center, Debby Davison, Anchor KEYT, Captain Chris Callahan-Dudley, Judge George Eskin, D.D.A.'s Mary Barron and Desmond McIntosh, Dr. Paul Willis, Maris Goodstein, Stan Hatch, Sissy Teran, Kathryn Henebry, Suzie Hayes, Cathy Collins Janey Cohen, Kate Schwab, Fred Klein, Norma Allerhand, Debra Geiger, Chris D'arco, Ann "Sully" Sullivan, Nichole Callahan, and Rosemary Torres.

Each of the people mentioned above really cares about "getting it right." Hence, their passion inspired me, and fills these pages.

1

Sound byte – Short extract from a recorded interview, chosen for its pungency.

Jordon grabbed the remote, aimed it at the kitchen TV, and pushed down on the power button.

The sound came on seconds before the picture.

"On Behalf of the People of the State of California, I ask that you find *this* malicious arsonist, **guilty** of the crime of first degree murder."

The image on the TV set changed from inside the courtroom to a close-up of Reporter Tina Lyle.

"That was Santa Barbara County District Attorney Jordon Danner concluding her closing argument while pointing at the Defendant Alexandra West. Once completed, Danner sat down, but not before making sure her lead investigator, A.T.F. agent Jake Manchester, displayed their final slide. Projected on the seven foot screen was a picture of the victim, Ruth Gold. The photograph was taken on her last birthday. Prominently displayed on the cake were the numerals seven and two, along with the same number of blazing candles. The candles' collective glow was dim in comparison with the smile on Miss Gold's face.

"For several seconds after the screen went blank the courtroom remained still, with the exception of a few jurors who wiped away tears.

"Ruthie, as most people called her, was a much beloved first-grade teacher. After she retired, she became one of the city's friendliest crossing guards. Her violent death devastated this community.

"The defendant, Alexandra West, is charged with setting fire to Miss Gold's house. Courtroom observers have told this reporter that the evidence presented at trial was entirely circumstantial and what little proof existed was heavily disputed.

"The jury deliberated most of today. At 4:30 this afternoon the foreman sent a note to the judge indicating they had reached a verdict. Given the late hour, Judge Ames ordered everyone back to court tomorrow morning at 8:30.

"Of course, KEYT news will be there for the reading of the verdict and we'll have a full report for you tomorrow on our five o'clock newscast.

"This is Tina Lyle, reporting live from the Santa Barbara Superior Courthouse, now back to you, Darcy, at our news center."

"Thanks, Tina. In other news tonight…"

***

"Bullshit!" Jordon bellowed. "What little proof there was…?" Tina," Jordon continued her one way dialogue with the kitchen TV, "there was *plenty* of proof!"

With each word spoken Jordon pounded harder on the raw chicken breast.

"And circumstantial evidence, *Tina,* is just as legally significant as direct evidence." Jordon's last hit nearly decimated her family's fowl.

Where is my family anyhow? Jordon wasn't expecting to see her three older sons tonight, but she thought at least her 16-year-old would be home. Sam, she now remembered, was at a play rehearsal and her husband Greg, she assumed, was still at work.

While stirring the boiling pot of pasta, Jordon thought about her husband and how rarely he seemed to *be there* for her these days or maybe, she considered, it was the other way around.

At 7:05, Jordon decided to eat dinner.

By 7:30, she'd already covered the remaining food.

Shortly after 8:00, while soaking in the bath, she listened as Greg arrived home. Moments later, she heard the sound of the microwave.

Eventually, Greg pushed on the mostly closed bathroom door. He walked in carrying a glass of wine in one hand and chicken *picatta* with shrimp-laced pasta in the other. Leaving the bathroom door mostly open, he put down his wine, lowered the toilet seat cover and sat down.

"So, how'd it go?" He asked, while appearing to search his pasta for the rare but coveted shrimp.

"Tina from Channel three said," Jordon raised her voice two octaves, "what little proof existed was heavily disputed."

"Sounds about right to me." Greg answered. "But that's why you're so good; you take a little bit of disputed proof and you spin it into solid evidence."

"I don't *spin* anything!" Jordon interrupted him. "I just present the facts to the jury as clearly as I can."

"Got it." Greg said.

Jordon wasn't sure if he was referring to a slippery shrimp, or her point. She thought Greg seemed oblivious to her intense reaction to both his choice of the word "spin" as well as the reporter's claim that Jordon only had "little proof." Sadly, she had no desire to pursue either misrepresentation any further with Greg.

"The important thing is," Greg continued, "this case from hell has finally ended, and since I heard on the radio you'll have your verdict tomorrow morning, you'll be done tomorrow afternoon. Then you'll be ready to take off with our boys on a much deserved, and much needed, sail!" Greg didn't wait for or seek Jordon's response. Instead he downed his wine and stood back up. "So, I'm going into the living room to watch the end of the Lakers game – can I get you anything?"

"No, thanks," she answered, "but please shut the bathroom door on your way out; it's getting a little cold in here."

Greg turned, flicked on the bathroom's heater, and quietly closed the door.

Jordon didn't question her love for Greg; still, she couldn't help but notice she felt less lonely after he left.

Soon the room's warmth returned, and with it, her overwhelming sense of guilt. Lying back in the tub, she closed her eyes and thought about Jake.

2

Friday, April 3, 2006 8:30 a.m.

Polling a jury – A practice whereby jurors are asked individually whether they assented, and still assent, to the verdict.

"We the jury in the above entitled action…"

Jordon didn't want to breathe; she was afraid she'd mishear the verdict.

"…hereby find…"

Why, Jordon wondered, did this part always take so long? She wanted to put her hand on Jake's leg. She knew she finally had her excuse - they'd been in this together for nearly two years. Even if anyone saw her do it, she rationalized; they'd just think under the circumstances it made sense.

"…the defendant, Alexandra West…"

Jordon put her hand down; her fingertips barely reached over to the inside of his thigh.

Jake placed his hand over hers.

"…guilty of the crime of first degree murder."

They each pressed down. Those were the very words every prosecutor and investigating officer longed to hear.

Jordon looked up at his perfectly-defined, closely-shaven jaw. Scrolling up his face, her gaze stopped at his soft blue eyes. "Jake," she whispered, "he did say guilty, right?"

Jake stared at the Foreman and barely responded, "Shhh."

Jordon kept staring at Jake. He finally gave her a slight smile.

Jordon heard a gasping sound. She turned to her right. Phillip Adler, the defense attorney, looked as if he'd just received an electrical shock. His body was suddenly rigid. Seconds later his shoulders and head dropped.

Phillip isn't doing it for effect, Jordon thought. He's devastated.

"Does either side," the judge asked, "wish the jury polled?"

Adler lifted his head, slid his elbows forward, and drew the microphone closer. In a barely audible voice he responded, "Yes, Your Honor."

Neither Jordon nor Jake let go. The judge began.

"Ladies and Gentlemen, first let me thank each of you for all your hard work. I know the deliberation process can be a difficult one. Still, I have one more procedure I'd like you to participate in. I am now going to do what is called – polling the jury. That is, I am going to ask each of you, individually, if the verdict just rendered is your personal, true and correct verdict. I will begin with Juror Number One. Ms. Vine, is that your true and correct verdict?"

"Yes, Your Honor." The young blonde UCSB co-ed nodded several times.

"Mr. Glick, is that your true and correct verdict?"

"It is, Your Honor." The middle-aged businessman responded, looking right into the judge's eyes.

"Mrs. White, is that your true and correct verdict?"

"Yes Sir," the aging Montecito widow whispered.

Jordon's olive skin began to reclaim its well-known glow as her hazel eyes started to glisten.

"Ms. Riley, is that your true and correct verdict?"

There was no answer.

Jordon's grip on Jake's leg tightened. Juror number four's lack of response sent a current of confusion through the courtroom. Five protracted seconds went by and no one spoke. Jordon could feel the defense team's spirit's rise. She crossed and re-crossed her long legs, while keeping her torso perfectly still. Jordon often called upon her years of dance training to make her appear more composed than she felt.

6

No one moved except Juror number four, Ms. Riley, who just looked down. When she looked back up her eyes were red.

Jordon began to panic. She had reservations about this juror right from the start. Like Jordon, Ms. Riley was a mother and a late "baby-boomer." Unlike Jordon, Ms. Riley chose to become a high school teacher. Jordon was concerned that the teacher in Ms. Riley might be too equivocal, but felt the mother in her would win out. Jordon expected Ms. Riley's maternal instinct to demand the streets be safer for her students and family. Jordon now feared the juror's theoretical side might, at least at the moment, be in control. Specifically, Jordon was fearful Ms. Riley could still be wrestling with the poorly written, and often confusing, legal concept of "reasonable doubt."

Judge Ames repeated his question. "Ms. Riley, is that your true and correct verdict?"

"No, Your Honor," she finally answered, "I mean, it might be. I just can't be certain, but everyone else seems so sure."

The judge interrupted her; his calm voice belied the frustration Jordon knew he felt. "Ms. Riley, I'm not asking you about anyone else. I'm asking you if the verdict of guilty is your *personal* verdict?"

Jordon looked up at Judge Ames. He was a handsome man, with a full head of dark hair. Recently, Jordon and most of the other lawyers in town attended a gala in honor of his 65th birthday. Back in the late 50's Ames was the lead singer of a popular folk music group. Even now, during this extremely tense moment, Ames still managed to maintain his smooth melodic voice, appealing manner, and uncanny ability to appear unflappable.

Jordon looked over at Ms. Riley, who was now looking up at the defendant. In that instant the juror's expression changed from concern to fear. Jordon turned and watched as Alexandra West held on to Ms. Riley's eyes and shamelessly willed her to stay the course. Ms. Riley finally looked away and turned to Judge Ames, her eyes now pleading with him to save her.

Judge Ames looked at Ms. Riley; his trained focus conveyed nothing. The juror bowed her head in humiliation. Her face reddened. She looked as if she wanted to disappear into her chair. Jordon wanted to strangle her.

"Ms. Riley," the judge finally announced, "I can see you are still deliberating, therefore, I shall ask you, and your fellow jurors, to return to the deliberation room. Mr. Foreperson, I will ask you to re-contact the bailiff if you have any further questions, comments, or if you've reached a *unanimous* decision. Finally," Ames said turning his attention to the entire jury, "I will remind all of you - to reach a verdict all twelve of you must be in agreement. That's all for now. We are in recess. My bailiff will give you further directions."

Judge Ames left the bench. All eyes turned to his bailiff, Deputy Ines.

Regina Ines was a middle-aged, blonde, beauty. She was also a part-time actress. Regina consistently appeared comfortable with the attention she always received. Regina walked over to the jury; everyone's eyes followed. She slowly placed both hands, each with five exceedingly long fingernails, over the railing. Leaning forward into the jury box, twisting her shoulders slightly, she began speaking to the jurors in hushed tones. Moments later the jurors stood and Regina led them back into the deliberation room. In spite of her obvious attempt to appease them, the jury still looked frustrated.

Neither Jordon nor Jake moved. A small pool of sweat formed between the palm of his hand and the back of hers. He gave her hand a quick squeeze and then lifted his momentarily-suctioned palm away.

Jordon released her grip on his leg and put her hands on her face. While rubbing her eyes she was careful to arch her fingers, she didn't want to let her nails scratch the bone beneath her brows. Jordon had scratched that place before, in other tense moments, and it always left her looking as if somebody had tried to scratch her eyes out, an image which enhanced her aggressive reputation, but not her undeniable beauty.

"Let's go," Jake said.

They stood up and walked toward the back of the courtroom. No one spoke. The defense team's glee was impossible to ignore; Jordon felt it like a dull knife being pushed between her shoulder blades.

Jordon knew everyone who stayed behind would take the bizarre turn of events personally. The clerk and bailiff would be disappointed that their plans to leave for an early lunch had been sabotaged. The court reporter would fear that without a guilty verdict, she might not get the extra money to prepare a transcript on appeal. The media would panic, not knowing how to interpret what had just occurred. Meanwhile, the observing defense attorneys would be glad-handing the defense team, while the remaining prosecutors would ache as if it had just happened to them. The judge, she guessed, would by now be on the phone with one of his colleagues expressing his greatest fear - that the jury would hang and he'd have to "try this damn case again."

Jordon, followed by Jake, stormed out the courtroom door. Without exchanging a word or look they turned left; they each knew where to go.

The stillness of the cavernous corridor was shattered by the sound of Jordon's high heels as they pounded on the courthouse tile floor and reverberated off its old adobe walls. Meanwhile, Jake's soft-soled paramilitary shoes remained silent.

"This," Jordon pronounced, "does not bode well for us."

"I know," he said, softening his voice and hoping she'd do the same.

"I mean," she continued, "*that woman* could really dig in."

***

Jake could hear the venom in Jordon's voice, but he knew if he turned toward her, he'd see nothing but fear. Best to keep my focus forward, he thought, at least for the moment. I sure as hell can't console her here.

"And," Jordon's voice began to rise, "she could drag others down with her."

Jake stopped and turned toward her. "Jordon, how about we just wait to talk until we get outside?"

***

Ever the Alcohol, Tobacco, and Firearms Agent, Jordon thought. He's always in control.

As they turned a corner, Jake moved in front of her; Jordon knew he did it out of protectiveness. When it came to Jake, she not only tolerated this chauvinist-appearing behavior, she understood and appreciated it.

Soon after they met Jordon learned Jake's passion to protect others was at the core of who he was. At 6'4"tall, 12 years her junior, but her equal in every other way, Jake always made Jordon feel both understood and safe.

They turned the next corner with the precision of synchronized swimmers and the grace of athletes. During her college years she pursued a double major in dance and pre-law, while he repeatedly medaled on his university's ski team. These days they both ran long distances.

Jake pushed the elevator button and, as expected, the door opened immediately; neither one of them was accustomed to waiting. He pressed "5." Once the door fully shut, Jake let down his guard. Stepping back, he closed his eyes and then banged the back of his head on the elevator wall.

At first the sound startled Jordon. Seconds later all she could think about was pressing her body against his; Jordon was sure he wanted that too. Still, she hesitated, and soon the elevator stopped. When its door opened, he extended his forearm, and she strode through.

Now in the vestibule, Jordon grabbed the cold door knob and pulled. This brief contact sent a chill through her wrist, and up to the inside of her elbow. She walked into the stairwell's entry. A moment later she felt a breeze as the door shut behind Jake. The chill continued up her arm, on to her neck and down her spine. Suddenly, the familiar stagnant, freezing air surrounded them. As Jordon mounted the steps, she could feel Jake's warmth coming from behind her. Once she reached the top, she pushed hard on the last barricade, an antiquated steel fire door. At last they were on the roof of the old courthouse, greeted by the heat of the morning sun.

Jordon briefly closed her eyes and took a deep breath. Exhaling, she opened them and headed to the right for her ocean view. Predictably, Jake veered to the left to gaze at his mountains. They each wanted a minute to gather their private thoughts. They often thought alike, and both knew the other needed to - check in with them self, before they spoke.

It was the first time Jordon had been away from him since they were summoned to court for the anticipated early-morning verdict. Jordon was still in shock. She'd expected finality, but instead was hurled into purgatory. Jordon was ready for victory or defeat, but not this uncertainty. She felt out of control, and hated feeling that way, especially when he was around.

Now watching the enormous ocean waves, she felt powerless; in the distance she saw white caps.

***

Jake was worried. While everyone else focused on Juror Number Four, he'd surveyed the remaining eight jurors. He thought when Ms. Riley spoke; he saw some of the others nod their heads in agreement. Jake decided not to tell Jordon what he'd observed. He was sure she was stressed out enough already.

Jake looked over at his Jordon. She's beginning to look skinny, still gorgeous as ever, but I think she's over-exercising and under-eating. She needs this, *all* of this, to be over. Jordon hates purgatory.

11

Over the past twenty months, Jake had never so much as kissed her; he would never kiss another man's wife, and until now, he'd never fallen in love with one.

"Hey, JoJo," only he and her husband called her that, "not planning on jumping are you? I mean I know you're able to leap tall buildings in a single bound, but I'm not so sure you can fly, too."

Jordon looked away. "And, I'm not so sure you think I can leap tall buildings in a single bound anymore. I just might have screwed this whole thing up."

Jake hoped he appeared as indignant as he felt. "We both know you didn't. We knew going into this it was a case based upon circumstantial evidence - a five hundred piece puzzle, as you told the jury. We both just hoped they'd be clever enough to put it all together and so far many of them have."

Jordon looked up. "What do you mean?" In an instant her tone of voice changed from fragile to frightened. "*Many* of them?"

Damn, Jake thought, she doesn't miss a thing, why did I have to put it that way? And now it would be useless for me to try and bullshit her. "Okay," he exhaled, "so while you were concentrating on Juror Number Four, I was watching the others. I'm afraid it looked to me like some of them…"

***

"Oh," she quickly surmised, "than we're screwed." Jordon felt her face drain and her eyes fill with tears. Jake stepped forward and took her in his arms.

First Jordon pictured Ruthie burning in the fire-ravaged room. Then she imagined the defendant standing a safe distance away, laughing, enjoying the blaze and the devastation it would cause. Jordon buried her face in Jake's warm neck. She tried to breathe him in, but found it hurt too much to breathe; she gasped and then sobbed. Jordon desperately wanted to bring Ruthie justice.

3

Friday, April 3, 2006 10:30 a.m.

Mistrial – A trial ending inconclusively.

Nearly two hours later, everyone was called back to court. Jake was right, the jury was now hopelessly hung, 8-4 for guilty, and all 12 felt it would be a waste of time to keep deliberating. The jury was dismissed.

After spending five months together in trial, the jurors quietly picked up their belongings and left. Their expressions told it all. They felt as if they'd failed; failed themselves, each other, and above all, a former stranger they'd all come to care for - a benevolent first grade teacher named Ruthie.

"Well, Ms. Danner," Judge Ames asked, once the courtroom had cleared, "how would you like to proceed?"

Jordon stood up and immediately started to feel woozy. She refused to appear vulnerable, and transferred her weight to her hands, pressing down on the table in front of her. "Your Honor…," she said, fingertips reddening, "this being Friday I'd like to continue the matter until Monday, if that is acceptable to the Court and counsel."

"Fine with us," Adler said, springing to his feet.

"All right," the judge agreed, "but, Ms. Danner, let me remind you, I do expect you to start <u>*People v. Cantera*</u> in about a month's time. Remember, *that* matter can't be delayed."

Jordon didn't respond. As the District Attorney, she felt it was inappropriate for any judge to point out either her duties or provisions of the Penal Code; including those which dictated priority for rape cases.

In an instant, Judge Ames seemed to realize his *faux pas*; appearing momentarily flustered, he turned his attention to the defendant. "Ms. West, I assume your lawyer has explained all of this to you. Because all twelve members couldn't agree, this jury did not reach a verdict. It's what we call a "hung jury." Therefore I have discharged them, and declared this to be a mistrial. Now the next step is likely up to Ms. Danner, who will decide whether to re-try this case, offer you a plea bargain, or dismiss the charges altogether. Ms. Danner has asked to continue this matter until Monday."

Alexandra West began to speak. Adler pressed down on his client's shoulder. West glared at him, arched her spine, and flicked back a clump of her graying hair.

Jordon turned away. Throughout the course of the trial, Alexandra West was repeatedly described by the media as appearing "indignant." While Judge Ames continued to address his comments to West, Jordon remembered a quotation she'd read about the defendant:

"At every conceivable opportunity, Ms. West makes it abundantly clear that *she* is the victim of a terrible miscarriage of justice. First, her favorite great aunt dies in a tragic fire; then she is falsely accused of joyfully setting that fire; next, she has to endure the indignity of living behind bars, and finally the public humiliation of a trial."

When Jordon first read that quotation she wasn't sure what the reporter believed, and now she didn't care; the jury had spoken.

"...Ms. West," Judge Ames concluded, "if you have any questions about what I've just said, please take them up with Mr. Adler. That's it for now. I will see all of you Monday morning at eight-thirty. I hope everyone has a pleasant weekend."

As soon as Judge Ames left the bench, Jordon stood and flipped her briefcase shut. "A pleasant weekend...? Hah!" Then turning to her friend Jan, the courtroom clerk, she added, "I was supposed to go sailing with the family to Santa Cruz Island; instead, I'll be going up to the damn mountain house alone."

"I thought," Jan asked, "you loved your place up there, as much as we love ours in Maui?"

"I do, it's just that last weekend we noticed how overgrown the trees were getting, so it's dark, and I'll be there alone - working. This *really* stinks!"

"I'm sorry," Jan said, "about your weekend *and* the verdict. Both should have gone your way."

"Thanks friend." Jordon smiled, exhaled, and turned.

By the time Jordon got to the back of the courtroom she was again seething.

***

Jake followed a safe distance behind her. He knew, at the moment that was all the nearness she could tolerate.

Jordon strode across the street and into the D.A.'s building. As she passed the offices of several of her colleagues, a few stuck their heads out and asked what had happened. Jordon kept walking.

The Assistant D.A., Rick Cohn, stepped out into the hallway and blocked her way. "So?"

Ooh, Jake thought, bad move. Rick, don't try and stop her now.

Jordon pushed Rick out the way and kept going.

No surprise there, Jake observed. I better run interference. "Hey Rick, why don't you and I go into your office for a minute?"

As Jake followed Rick into his office, Jordon flashed Jake an unambiguous glance of outrage. Boy, Jake thought, those hazel eyes can get fiery.

***

Jordon ripped into her office and slammed the door shut. The ensuing boom was doubtlessly heard throughout the building. Jordon hadn't slammed a door since she'd been in junior high. But this is too much, she thought. First I have to watch my case go down the toilet and then, suddenly, Jake disappears on me!

Jordon sat down, then immediately shot back up and began to pace. Moments later, she heard his knock. Jordon sat back down. "Come in," she said without emotion.

Jake pushed his head in, but left the rest of his body on the other side of the door. "Is it safe?" he asked.

"Yes, of course it's *safe*."

Jake stepped in, closed the door behind him, but didn't move any closer.

"So," she asked, trying to act as if she were engrossed in some insignificant paperwork, "why'd you leave me to talk to *him?*"

Jake raised his eyebrows and cocked his head. "Because, *he* is one of *your* best friends and *he* actually gives a shit about *you* and *our* case. And," he added, starting out sounding defensive but ending up sounding loving, "I talked to him, so you wouldn't have to."

In an instant, Jordon knew Jake was right and she was acting like a brat. "I'm sorry," her voice dropped. "So then tell me," she said, momentarily averting her eyes, "why do you put up with me?"

"Because," he answered smiling, "I think you can leap tall buildings in a single bound," and, he thought, because I'm in love with you. "But hey," he quickly added, "no apology necessary, you're exhausted. As usual, you've given this case your all. So why don't you just sit down, I'll get us a couple of bottles of water then I'll come back, shut the door and won't leave again until you're sick of me." Jake gave her upper arm a quick squeeze and left.

Getting sick of him, she thought, was one thing she was sure could never happen.

While Jake was gone, Jordon cleared off her desk. As soon as he returned, they shared the desk and started working on their lists.

An hour later someone knocked at the door; they sprang apart.

"Lunch time," Rick bellowed. He was carrying two turkey sandwiches prepared just the way he knew they liked them - extra mayo for Jake, dry for Jordon. "Work all you want, you two, but you've *got* to eat."

Jordon took the sandwiches, put them down, and threw her arms around Rick. While she hugged him she quietly apologized. Rick responded with his own apology, whispering he should have known better than to get in her face at that particular moment.

Rick and Jordon had been friends from the moment they met 15 years ago. They had one of those often sought after, rarely obtained, male-female friendships. Theirs was a friendship full of respect and absent confusing sexual overtones. They simply revered each other and would never let the other down, or intentionally interfere with the other's right to be cranky and self-centered, especially when in trial.

Jordon watched as Rick laid out their sandwiches and folded napkins. Rick was just over 6 feet tall and weighed close to 180 pounds. He had been a serious hiker, but lately had taken to ocean rowing and kayaking. With his thick light brown hair and seductive smile, most women watching his trials, reporters and courtroom observers alike, couldn't keep their eyes off him. Between his looks, warmth, intelligence, and compassion, many found him irresistible even before he gave his closing argument. Once he gave his closing, they were all his.

It made Jordon smile, thinking of all the times Rick concurrently charmed a jury and a reporter. Sadly, none of those infatuations lasted, and consequently, Jordon was still on the look-out for the woman of his dreams.

As Rick stood back to admire the lunch setting he'd just created, Jordon again considered how someday he'd make some very lucky woman very happy.

"So," Rick asked, "how much longer are you two gonna process this?"

Jordon glanced up at her wall clock. "Only another hour or so. I promised Greg and the boys I'd go down to the dock to see them off." Jordon always felt strange saying her husband's name in front of Jake. "I was *supposed* to go with them," Jordon told Rick, "but now, I'll be working instead."

"Hey pal," Rick looked painfully sincere, "I am really sorry. I wish I could help, but I know I can't. No one knows this case better than you. But remember I'm just a phone call away all weekend if you need *anything*." Rick paused for a moment to make sure Jordon knew he meant it. Then, turning to Jake, he asked, "And what are you up to?"

Jordon sat down and busied herself with meaningless documents, while she wondered if Rick sensed there was something going on between her and Jake.

"I'm going to stick around Santa Barbara for the weekend," Jake answered. "Jordon and I have come up with a few things I need to do to prepare for Monday's hearing. After that, I'll be returning to Washington. Then, depending upon what Jordon decides, I'll either be back next month for the retrial or..."

"What do you mean," Jordon lifted her head and interrupted, "what I decide? I thought we were in this together?"

"Hey," Jake came right back at her, "I'm here to support you. You did a brilliant job in there. I can't imagine you doing any better a second time around, but if you want to roll the dice again - I'll be there with you."

Their eyes locked.

"Okay," Rick said temporarily shattering their bond, "I'm outta here. The love-fest between the two of you always makes me feel like a third wheel." Rick took Jordon's face into his hands, kissed her cheek, and left.

Maybe, Jordon considered, Rick doesn't suspect anything. If he did, he's not likely to tease us. But knowing Rick that could just be his way of saying *back off.* Rick was the best trial lawyer Jordon knew. He had a way of convincing juries to think the way he did, while making them feel as if it were their idea all along. Either way, Rick's impression of Jake and me will have to wait for another day; there's too much going on today already.

"Is there any chance," Jake asked, "Rick feels weird about me because I'm black?"

"No, no chance at all," Jordon answered. "Rick has tremendous respect for you. What he feels weird about - is us. I'm guessing he's picking up on something, some sort of vibe between us, but he doesn't want to believe it, and so he's trying not to."

Jake's voice softened as he leaned toward her. Jordon could feel his warm breath on her neck. "So are you picking up on some sort of *vibe* between us?"

Always, she thought. "Nope," she said swatting him with her legal pad. "We now have fifty-two minutes left before I leave, and I want to make sure we've got all our bases covered."

"Okay Coach," he smiled, "what's next?"

They easily slipped back and forth between the various roles they played in their multi-faceted relationship; it was one of the things she liked best about them.

***

Fifty one minutes later, Jake stood up. "Okay, now I'm outta here. I've got my list and your weekend phone number," Jake looked over at her and bowed, "everything I need to slay a dragon for my lady. Wish me luck. I'll call you after my visit to the jail." Jake turned, hesitated, turned back and asked, "Okay if I leave now?" His smile lit up her face.

No, she thought. "Yes," she said smiling back.

Jake stepped forward and kissed her cheek. Jake's kiss took half the time of Rick's, but the sensation lasted until he shut the door behind him.

Suddenly Jake was gone, and just as suddenly, she missed him, especially because she could still hear his voice as she listened to him say his good-byes to Rick. Don't *go there*, Jordon admonished herself; there's work to be done.

Now, temporarily distracted from her roller-coaster of emotions, Jordon focused instead on what she wanted to bring. She had to make sure she had all the material she needed to work on both the <u>West</u> and <u>Cantera</u> cases.

Driving the five minutes over the hill toward the ocean, Jordon felt completely schizophrenic. She loved her husband, but was infatuated with Jake. She was always quick to condemn other women in her situation, but now she felt hypocritical and dishonest. Several of her friends had affairs, but Jordon knew she could never do that. Jordon had too much respect for Greg, but she wanted to be with Jake, especially when Greg touched her. Later, she thought, I'll sort it all out later. For now, I'm going to focus on my family.

***

Jordon reached the dock and saw them in the distance. Struck by the intensity of her feelings of love and guilt, she rushed toward them. She slowed her pace just before arriving.

George, her handsome and lanky 26-year-old son, was bent over the boat's motor. Jordon snuck up on him and placed her arms around his waist. He didn't budge. "Hi Mom." His voice was calm and full of warmth.

"Working hard, big guy?" she asked.

"Just checking on the new fuel filters."

"Oh good, you put in new fuel filters." They both smiled; each knowing she had no idea what he was talking about. "So, does that make the boat safer?" Jordon asked, as she came around in front of him.

"Ever the *mutha*," George smiled and rubbed her head. "Don't know, but it should make it go a little faster, which is exactly what we need right now because it's *really* not cool for us to be leaving this late in the day for the islands."

"Then let's go!" Sam offered as he approached the group. "Hey, Mom!"

As soon as Sam arrived he wrapped Jordon in his muscular arms; smashing her face into his chest. Sam's hug made it difficult for Jordon to breathe, but she'd never push him away. Sam was her baby, and she'd take every last hug he had to offer. Sam continued talking, apparently oblivious to her breathing difficulties. "Hey Mom, it's a bummer you're not going with us." He finally let go. "Gotta work, huh?"

Sam was trying to appear adult-like with his question and concern, but Jordon knew as much as he loved her, it really didn't matter to Sam if Jordon went; what mattered to him was *when* they'd finally get going. Without waiting for her response, Sam pushed a handful of sun-streaked blonde hair out of his face and looked around for his father.

Jordon missed the platinum curls of Sam's youth. Now at 16, and 6' 1", Sam towered over her 5' 6" frame. Although Jordon still thought Sam was gorgeous, she now believed he looked more like a classic California surfer than the Little Lord Fauntleroy of their not-so-distant past. Jordon was glad Sam had recently given up football and was pursuing his interest in theater and politics. Sam said he did it because he wanted to use his natural good looks and charm, rather than destroy them. No one disagreed, but it wouldn't have done them any good if they had: Sam, like her other three sons, was strong-willed, passionate, and confident, sometimes to his detriment. Jordon smiled as she thought, what is it they say about apples not falling too far from their trees?

"Wait a minute, you guys." Greg said coming up from the boat's galley. "Maybe we should stick around and have lunch with your mother. I think she's had a very rough morning and is in for a very long, hard, weekend." Greg worked his way between their sons and put his arm around his wife. Their sons looked crestfallen. They were ready to go.

"Thank you, sweetheart," Jordon responded, patting his hand with hers, "but I'm okay Rick brought me lunch while I was getting organized." Jordon decided not to say 'brought *us* lunch.' "Anyway, I've got a ton of work to do and I should get up to The Log before it gets dark. And,

George says you guys should set sail before it gets any later."

Jordon tried to look concerned instead of confused. After 27 years of marriage she feared the slightest lowering of her guard might transmit something that would raise Greg's angst. She hoped if Greg sensed anything, he'd just chalk it up to her stressful morning.

"Right... Okay..." Greg said, looking as if he was being pulled in two directions; just the way Jordon felt. "Well," he concluded, "I'll miss you."

Jordon put her arms around him and gave him a tight hug. She couldn't say she'd miss him too. Between all the work she had to do, and her feelings toward Jake, Jordon knew she needed to be away from Greg, at least for this weekend. As Jordon pulled away she thought she caught a glimpse of Greg's hurt feelings, but she knew he wouldn't push it - he never did.

"Well, don't work too hard," Greg offered.

"Define 'too hard,'" Jordon said stepping back and smiling.

"Okay, Counselor, let me rephrase that," Greg's smile answered hers, "don't forget to eat and sleep. For my part, I shall bring you back two handsome sailors and a killer calico bass. I'm just sorry you and the other boys couldn't join us. Speaking of the other guys, have you heard from them?"

"Yep, I had a voicemail from them when I got to work. It was six a.m. and they were just leaving La Jolla." Jordon shook her head and grinned. She was glad their other two sons, Anthony and Ray, had gone to San Diego for a few days. Anthony always loved visiting his old friends there, especially if he could bring Ray with him.

Jordon smiled as she thought of Ray. Ray was the one son all of her other sons always got along with. He was the first to help any of them with their homework or any other project, and he often did so at his own expense. Ray was highly intelligent, gentle, kind, and above all else - fun. He had red hair, freckles, and forest green eyes. Ray could be counted on to be the first one to dance at a party and the loudest to shout out one of his brothers names when they were a participant at any event. Still, as much as Jordon admired Ray, what endeared him to her was his smile. Whenever Ray smiled at her she felt as if she were butter - melting in his warmth.

Jordon knew if he and Anthony were together, they were watching out for each other and having fun.

"So, I'm guessing," Greg offered looking at his watch, "Ray and Anthony are still asleep and safe?"

"Honey, they are twenty-four and twenty-three years old. They are spending the weekend partying in San Diego; safety is not their greatest concern. Face it, we've lost control." They laughed the laugh of an old married couple, Jordon found it comforting. "Please," she asked, "just take care of yourself, George, and Sam."

After saying her final good-byes, Jordon watched them load on the last of their provisions and pull away from the dock. With her throat nearly closed, she still managed to eke out a nearly inaudible, "I love you all." In spite of her best efforts to keep it together, she became teary; she knew she should be in the same boat as her family, instead of watching them sail away.

Jordon returned home, gathered some food, her two bulldogs – Brutus and Caesar and drove away in the CRV. Although the car was mostly full of boxes of evidence, tapes, and files, her dogs still managed to make themselves comfortable.

Jordon was finally on her way to their mountain home, where she knew she had a whole lot of thinking to do.

4

Friday, April 3, 2006 5:00 p.m.

"You can't always get what you want, but if you try sometime, you just might find, you get what you need."
Rolling Stones

A few hours later, Jordon was 4,000 feet above Santa Barbara, and 10 minutes away from their second home. She was slowly approaching the most dramatic part of the road.

Jordon always looked forward to this transition, it reminded her of the feeling she got each night in Santa Barbara when she came home from work and switched from high-heels to slippers. Just around the next bend, she thought, the low desert terrain will transform into tall pine trees.

As Jordon gained elevation, the sky began to darken.

Suddenly snowflakes were whirling in front of her headlights. In her present state, the onslaught of snow seemed like nothing short of an omen. One of her favorite CDs was playing – Lionel Ritchie's, "True Love Songs." Jordon knew she should be thinking of Greg, but all she could do was fantasize about Jake. She longed to be sharing this moment with him. Jordon reached out and picked up her cell phone. I shouldn't, she decided. Not wanting to be enticed she tossed the phone into the back seat, almost hitting poor Brutus, and then she increased her speed.

Once again, Jordon's throat began to close - the precursor of inevitable tears. Jordon was feeling drawn toward Jake, and it hurt. Jordon hated being in pain. She wanted to do what one of her theme songs from her college days told her to do, she wanted to - "love the one you're with" and not long for someone else. She also wanted to -"be in the here and now," as the famous 70's philosopher expounded, and not romanticize about what her life would be like with Jake. Jordon's head told her, choosing to be with Jake would not be good for her family or her career, but her heart constantly reminded her how much she wanted him. The Rolling Stones said it best, she decided: "You can't always get what you want, but if you try sometime, you just might find, you get what you need." But what she thought she needed most at this very moment was Jake.

All at once, the car began to skid on the icy road. Jordon panicked. She was suddenly in the lane of oncoming traffic.

The skid felt as if it would never end.

Finally, she was able to pull out of it, and onto the side of the road. As she rested her head on the steering wheel, she was sure she could hear her own heart pounding. "Jordon, you idiot," she berated herself, "you've got to be more careful, you've got four sons." Caesar leapt over the seat and put his head in her lap.

Still trembling, Jordon pushed the "EJECT" button on the CD player. No more mind-altering music, she thought; I need a little mindless, upbeat…maybe a little… Yeah, she decided, finding *Yellow Submarine,* I need Beatle music.

Getting back on the road she started to feel more in control, until the song *Yellow Submarine* was replaced by *Nowhere Man.* "…making all his nowhere plans for nobody…"

So, if I'd gotten into a car accident, she began to fantasize, I wonder if I would've had my excuse to call Jake. Chastising herself yet again, she put a halt to that particular delusion, and instead, drove the remaining five minutes without music, and with caution.

When Jordon first pulled into her driveway, the house and surrounding area was dark, smothered in overgrown trees. In a flash, the motion sensing lights came on. It created a welcoming glow on their three-story, six-bedroom log home. Jordon decided to sit in her car for a moment.

She wanted to watch snowflakes fall under the lit branches. Brutus began to lick her face and frantically jumped between the back and the front seats; he wanted to get away and play in the snow. Jordon opened the door and the dogs tumbled out, tripping all over themselves and anything else in their way. Seconds later, they were gone, but Jordon could still hear them yapping in the empty lot next door. Confident they were safe, she turned her attention back to the view. Jordon had never dreamed she'd own a house this remote or this grand.

Jordon grew up in New York City, the granddaughter of Jewish immigrants and the daughter of working class parents. Her grandparents began homeless. Her parents never owned their own home, and now Jordon owned two. Because of her family's hard work and generosity, Jordon was able to stay in school. For that reason, and many others, she never took her prosperity for granted, nor did she ever let herself forget that her privileged circumstances came at great cost to those who came before her.

When Jordon was ready to go in, she called for the dogs and together they entered the house through the downstairs side door. From there, she walked directly into her bedroom. The strong scent of the old pine logs comforted her. It was what had convinced her to buy the house five years ago. Jordon remembered walking into the house for the first time and immediately whispering to Greg, "Smells like home." Greg took her hand then, and gave it a loving squeeze. Jordon usually smiled when she thought of that moment, but she didn't smile today. Now as she went into their bathroom to splash cold water on her face, she saw her image in the mirror. I look as old and as tired as I feel, she thought. The cold water, followed by the thick, soft terry-cloth, calmed her. Jordon kept the towel pressed up against her nose and took a deep breath. Even the laundry, she thought, smelled better in the mountains.

Returning the towel to the rack, she glanced over at the double shower with its royal blue and white tile. Standing there, she briefly imagined how erotic it would be to shower with Jake. A moment later, she chastised herself for letting that thought sneak through.

As she lifted her arm to turn off the bathroom light, she felt exhausted and overwhelmed. All the ups and downs of the day had finally caught up with her. Her bed looked enticing. But, I can't stop now, she thought.

She returned to the car, and grabbed a few file boxes. Once back inside, she dropped them on the bed. On her last trip out, she gathered the small bag of groceries and took it upstairs to the kitchen. The dogs followed, with obvious hopes of getting a treat.

The kitchen smelled clean, but felt too big and very empty. This was the room where everyone congregated and got in her way. Today, the absence of family and friends made it seem almost eerie. Jordon put the bag down on the tiled center island and took note of its puny contents. Usually, upon her arrival, she was unloading boxes of groceries - everything she needed for making grand and bountiful meals. Today, she put away salad fixings, two cans of tuna, a small bag of hard Granny Smith apples and a package of soft mozzarella cheese. When she opened a low cabinet, Brutus barked with joy while Caesar sat down and tried to appear perfectly behaved; within that cupboard were the dog biscuits. They both received their treats, smiled, and toddled away.

After cutting up an apple and some cheese, Jordon discovered a box of not-too-stale crackers, opened a bottle of Pinot Noir, and found her beloved wine glass. The glass bore the inscription "Ahwanee," her family's favorite hotel. Don't go *there* either, she thought. She placed everything on a tray, and returned to the stairway.

As she walked down the steps, she missed everyone and dreaded the work she was about to do. Jordon had expected to be done with the <u>West</u> case by now. Instead, she was going to have to read through everything in the hopes of finding anything. Jordon was looking for some small nugget of information which would convince her to either re-try the case, offer a plea-bargain, or dismiss the charges altogether.

As she set the tray down on her bed, she just hoped that nugget existed.

Feeling the chill of the evening mountain air, especially downstairs, Jordon decided to light the bedroom's cast iron stove. While waiting for the flames to grow, she wandered into the adjacent room.

The room next to their bedroom was a personal gym, replete with every necessary piece of workout equipment. Jordon got on the stationary bike to both warm up and, as she used to tell her children, emancipate her endorphins. It was going to be a long night.

After pedaling for a few moments, she returned to put a larger piece of wood on the fire. As she opened the side-loading door, Jordon was greeted by a wave of warm air and charmed by the fledging fire's beauty. Once the piece of wood was secured, she walked toward her bed. As she climbed up, she was careful not to tip over the brightly colored tray or the bruised and coffee-stained file boxes. While balancing on her knees, she poured a half glass of wine and put a slice of apple in her mouth. Next she arranged the over-stuffed pillows and seized her notebook from the top of the box. At last, she sat back, opened the notebook, and began to chew. Soon the pups settled by her side.

Suddenly the phone rang.

Jordon flinched. The pups took off. The ring seemed loud and out of place. Maybe it's Jake, she hoped. After spitting the apple pieces in the nearby wastepaper basket; she took a gulp of wine and answered the phone.

"Jordon Danner," she announced in her most provocative professional tone.

"Well, who the hell else besides Jordon Danner would be up in that God-forsaken log cabin?"

Jake's voice added color to the entire room, especially to her face.

"Just me and the chipmunks, but sometimes they get to the phone first and I have a heck of a time wrestling it away from them."

"Well," his pitch dropped an octave as his pace slowed, "would you like me to come up and help?"

She knew he meant it, so she didn't take his question seriously. "*I'd* love the company, but the chipmunks, that's another story. They are a very jealous lot with a pack mentality, and you don't want to stroll through their territory."

"Hell, I'd march through a valley of vicious chipmunks just to be with you."

Jordon could just picture his cocky smile and glistening eyes. "My hero." She had to change both the tone and subject of their conversation; they were on dangerous ground. "So, whatcha got?"

"I'm not sure yet," Jake took on her business-like manner. "Alexandra made three calls from her jail cell. One to a distant cousin, just a bunch of whining, one to her gardener, and one to what sounded like an old acquaintance."

"So, you already listened to the calls?"

"Yep."

"And?"

"Well, nothing on the surface, but she did mention a few things I've never heard before. Someone on the outside patched her though to a woman named *Doreen*, who mentioned 'that *Sylvia* thing.' The other call was to Ming at Paradise Gardening. She's called Ming a time or two before, but this time they weren't just talking about her rose garden, they also talked about trees and a van, still gardening stuff though."

"So, that's it?" Jordon couldn't keep the disappointment out of her voice.

"That's it. No smoking gun, but still worth my time checking it out, no?"

Jordon had always been attracted to men who felt passionately about their work and Jake was no exception.

Jake's work ethic was one of the things she admired most about him, that and…

"Jordon, don't you agree?"

"Yeah, sorry, I agree." Jordon had just been thinking about how great Jake looked in 501 Levis and a white tee shirt. "We have to follow every possible lead. So, you're going to be working into the night?"

"Yep, same as you. I'll run both names in a variety of ways, who knows. I'd sure like to give you *something* new before Monday."

She knew he was teasing her with his suggestive comment, but thinking of him leaving on Monday made smiling impossible. Perhaps it's for the best, she thought. Deciding not to respond to either his tease or impending departure, she said, "Okay, well, I'll be up for hours - call me if you find something."

"Will do." He sounded disappointed. "So, are you okay up there? I checked the weather it looked like it might be snowing. It's pouring down here."

"I'm fine." Hearing about the rain made her think about the safety of her boys. I should call the Harbor Patrol, she thought. That distraction made it easier for her to hang up. "So, okay, I gotta go, call me later." She almost added a thoughtless, 'Miss you,' her guard temporarily down, but thankfully, she didn't.

Jordon called the Harbor Patrol.

Officer Eric Swenson assured her there had been no 'distress calls', and her son George could easily handle a storm that size. Still, he offered to take down her number and call her if there was any reason to worry.

Temporarily placated, Jordon went back to her plate of munchies and boxes of documents. Begin at the beginning, she concluded.

5

Thursday, August 17, 2004 4:03 p.m.

Arson – The malicious burning of a dwelling house.

"911. What is your emergency?"

"This is Judge Patel over at the Bankruptcy Court. There's a terrible fire in the house across the street."

"What is the address of the house on fire?"

"125 East Sola Street."

"Do you think anyone's inside?"

"No, a sweet old lady lives there, but I saw someone pick her up earlier. Even so, you must hurry. The fire is getting rather large and I'm afraid it's going to spread throughout the neighborhood."

***

Jordon later learned that was the moment Judge Patel dropped his phone and ran.

***

The calls which followed echoed Judge Patel's observations and sentiments.

According to the dispatch log, Santa Barbara Fire Department fire trucks arrived within four minutes. Upon their arrival, flames were shooting out of several structures. The most "involved" structures appeared to be a small house and the Federal Bankruptcy Court.

Fifteen minutes later, Battalion Chief Hess called in the arson investigation team. Hess wasn't at all sure he had an arson on his hands, but he didn't want to be accused of being flippant, especially if a federal building was involved. The on-call arson investigator was Mark Dickens.

Dickens was known as a big brash man with a similarly sized heart of gold. Dickens arrived within 30 minutes of being called. Standing back, watching the flames, it looked to Dickens as if the fire began in the small house, and spread from there. When Dickens thought it was safe he walked into that house. He was searching for the sources of ignition and the area of origin.

Within moments, Dickens was standing in a smoky, acrid-smelling bedroom. He sensed he wasn't alone. Underneath the remains of the bed he caught a glimpse of a small partially-shod foot. He crouched down.

Mark Dickens smelled the victim before seeing the rest of her body. It was the unmistakable, totally out-of-place smell of barbeque. One glance was enough. Standing up he swallowed back his nausea. A moment later, he turned and walked outside to call his supervisor, Todd Peterson.

Todd was a gentle man with soft brown eyes and sandy hair. Although he was about to turn 50, he looked as if he were still in his 30s. Mark and Todd had a few common goals which had, over the years, become passions. First, they had to figure out the cause of each fire they were called to. Then, if they decided it was an arson, they had to get the bad guy. However, no matter what their workload was, their own families always came first. To keep each other resolute in reaching these objectives, they became bickering best friends.

"Hello?" Todd answered.

"There's an 1144 in there."

Mark's declaration was followed by a moment of silence during which time both of them knew Mark gave the radio code for "dead body" with more bravado than he felt.

"How old?" Todd asked.

"Can't tell for sure, except to say it was an adult female."

"Easily identifiable?"

"Nah."

"So did the suppression team screw-up our scene?"

"Too soon to tell."

"Any reason to believe we've got an arson?"

"Nope, but no reason to disbelieve it either, and I'll tell ya there was nothin' on my quick walk-through that jumped out at me to say it was accidental."

"I'll be there in twenty minutes. Are you okay?"

"Yeah, sure, but that poor lady. Man she's really burnt up."

"Ok. Standby. Do you want video?"

Just then Todd overheard someone ask Mark, "So, where's the crispy critter?"

Mark didn't answer the questioner, but instead told Todd, "Not unless we got a video camera without a microphone. We still got a lot of noisy people hanging out here. I think it's safer just to go with straight photos; ya never know what some of these knuckle-heads will yell out while we're taping."

"Right," Todd answered. "I'll be there soon – take it easy."

***

By the time Todd arrived, the house the victim was found in was virtually destroyed. Meanwhile, two other homes, along with the Bankruptcy Court, sustained only partial damage. An hour later, deputies from the coroner's office arrived. At first, they took only photographs and measurements; eventually, they took the victim.

Long after everyone else left, five members of the Fire Investigation team were still working. One member of the team, Jack Allen, was memorializing the scene with photos and rudimentary sketches. The others were going through the rubble and ash, some by hand, others using screens.

After searching independently, they collectively concluded they couldn't find a single item capable of causing an accidental burn. Their fire scene, they surmised, was starting to look like a crime scene. Todd stepped outside to call the police.

Todd sat down under a blooming Jacaranda tree and spoke to his friend, Santa Barbara Police Department Detective Sergeant Mark Murray. Mark in turn called in his team: Detectives David McGraw and Larry Duran, along with Forensic Specialists Matt Stevens and Matt Underwood.

In an abundance of caution, McGraw requested a search warrant. Once the search warrant was secured, all nine investigators worked together for the next several hours. After completing their search, and systematically recording their findings, they began to interview everyone in the immediate neighborhood.

By dawn they began to pack up. As they left, each was sure of only two things: the fire was intentionally set, and because the bankruptcy court sustained significant internal damage, they needed to call an A.T.F. Agent. Todd's first choice was Agent Jake Manchester.

Manchester was an arson specialist who'd developed a reputation for his investigative talents. Tenacious was the word that came to Todd's mind, but relentless was probably more like it. Todd had worked with Jake in the past. Todd knew as soon as Jake arrived he'd take over the whole investigation, but under these circumstances, that was perfectly okay with Todd.

***

Jake Manchester was saddened by the death of yet another arson victim, but he felt honored to be summoned. Jake had enjoyed working with S.B.F.D. and S.B.P.D. in the past. Unlike most other law enforcement agencies, the Santa Barbara ones seemed to really appreciate his help and did whatever they could to support what soon became *his* investigation. Beyond that, Santa Barbara in the summer was much nicer than Washington D.C.

Jake landed 19 hours after the fire began. When he arrived, he went directly to the fire scene. After doing his own "walk through," he drove over to the Fire Department.

As soon as Todd saw Jake he gave him a warm greeting, a S.B.F.D. coffee mug and a small work space. Once Jake sat down, Todd rolled his chair over and they began to work. Of surprise to both of them was the fact that nearly 24 hours had passed and still no one had called inquiring about the victim. By then, the pathologist had already concluded she was an older woman, in all likelihood, Ruth Gold, the owner of the house.

The next day, Jake, along with several S.B.P.D. officers, went in search of family members. They needed to secure Ruth's dental records or X-rays. Everyone they contacted referred them to Alexandra West, the victim's great niece, and occasional caretaker. Jake called West and left multiple messages, but West never called back.

After 72 hours had passed, and willing to wait no longer, S.B.P.D. Detectives, along with Agent Manchester, went to West's apartment. They arrived the same time she did.

Detective McGraw later reported West's reaction to the news of her great aunt's death was "initially appropriate, but then," he went on to say, "her grief seemed short-lived" Further, "She seemed surprised and perhaps annoyed that a criminal investigation had been opened, and even asked, "Why can't you just let sleeping *dogs* lie?" According to McGraw the only thing Alexandra seemed to bemoan, and she did so over and over again, was that she'd let a week go by without even visiting her "dearly beloved" Aunt.

Toward the end of the interview, Alexandra asked if she could go to her Aunt's house to look through the rubble for a few personal articles. The detectives said she could, as long as they accompanied her. Once there, West took a moment to look around and then grabbed "a few, mostly burnt, knick-knacks".

Detective Duran lingered behind to document what she had taken while Detective McGraw and Agent Manchester drove her home.

As Detective Duran was about to step back into his car, an aristocratic Indian man in his late fifties approached him. "So, what'd she say?" he asked.

Detective Duran was caught off guard, "I'm sorry, who is she? And for that matter, who are you?"

"I'm, Judge Patel, the one who called 9-1-1 the day of the fire. And the *she*, that's the lady who was just here." Judge Patel paused, apparently waiting for Detective Duran to make the connection; when he didn't, Patel added, "she's the one I saw Ruthie leaving with that morning...that's why I thought Ruthie wasn't home."

Detective Duran tried not to show his delight. He didn't want it to come back at him during the trial. He never wanted to be accused of trying to influence a witness. Still, he could barely contain his excitement. He thought this might be their first break in a very important case. "Are you *sure* you saw *that* woman the morning of the fire?"

Patel looked bewildered by the question. "Positive, only she wasn't in her usual car; she was in a kind of minivan. It looked like a rental."

"Did it have a particular rental car logo?"

"Not that I recall, well, yes, maybe Budget was written on the license plate holder, but I'm not really sure."

"Did you know Ruthie well enough to know if she had any visitors on a regular basis?"

"Yes and no, I mean I knew her, and no, she didn't have many visitors as of late...but she used to. She only retired a few years ago from her last job. First, she was a teacher, for about thirty years I think. Matter of fact she was my daughter's teacher – Ruthie Gold was great with the kids; so warm and supportive."

Patel sighed, looked down and shook his head. After an awkward moment, he continued. "Right after she retired she became a crossing guard."

It appeared to Detective Duran that Judge Patel needed to talk. Duran had important work to do, but it would have to wait. Duran believed listening patiently to grief-stricken community members was also an important part of his job.

"Ruthie told me once," Patel offered, "a couple of years ago, when she was still a crossing guard, that she hadn't slept too well the night before because she was trying to think of something to say to the children. That's when she first told me she always tried to start the kid's days off right. She felt it was her job while taking them across, to say something unique and sincere to each one of them – something new every day." Patel swallowed. "Ruthie Gold was a lovely woman." He paused again and shook his head. "A few years ago, her knees gave out and she had to retire. I think that about killed her. At first people came to visit her all the time, but eventually, I guess the older she got, the less people felt comfortable being around her, soon they stopped coming all together. And she never did marry, so her only relatives were her sister's family." Patel's eye reddened. "I should have been a better neighbor." This time, when Patel dropped his head, he left it there.

"Your Honor," Duran said, reaching out to touch Patel's shoulder.

Judge Patel looked up.

"I'm sorry for your loss."

Judge Patel waved Detective Duran off. It appeared to Duran the Judge was embarrassed by his emotional reaction.

"I'm just sorry," Patel responded, "that I didn't save Ruthie."

"Sir," Duran offered, "from what I understand, she'd already died by the time the flames were visible.

Judge Patel seemed somewhat relieved.

After thanking him, Duran left.

As soon as he could, Duran called McGraw on his Nextel. "Are you guys still with Miss West?"

"Yeah, why?" McGraw asked.

Duran's heart was sprinting. "Where are you?"

"Her place. Why, what's going on?"

"Is she nearby?"

"Sort of."

"Don't make her suspicious, and above all, don't leave."

"Oh," McGraw responded, "we're just looking though some of Ruthie's old pictures."

It sounded to Duran as if McGraw was starting to get it. "Good. Stay there. I'll be there in less than five minutes. Tell her I'm coming over. Then I'll wait at the door until she *invites* me in. I don't want any damn attorney telling me I needed a warrant. Just follow my lead."

Minutes later, Duran arrived and as hoped, Alexandra West invited him in.

Within moments Duran confronted her.

Although Alexandra appeared flustered at first, she soon admitted she had lied and had seen her aunt that day. Then she claimed she had rented the van for Ruthie's comfort, and took her to a champagne brunch. Finally, she said she snuck Ruthie back in the back door because she drank too much champagne and Alexandra knew Ruthie wouldn't want the neighbors to see her drunk.

The Detective's questioning continued.

***

Jake noted every time West was asked a direct question, she gave an evasive response. Finally, when Duran asked her more about the van, suggesting she rented the van in the hopes of not being remembered, West became indignant and asked for a lawyer. Having made that legally significant request, all further questioning ceased.

West was then brought down to the jail, photographed, fingerprinted and booked.

Upon leaving the jail, each investigating officer was *confident* they had probable cause to arrest Alexandra West.

They just hoped more evidence would develop or they *knew* she'd soon be released.

***

Jordon put down the initial reports and took a look at what the rest of the investigation had developed.

The autopsy results showed Ruthie Gold had a blood alcohol level of 0.16 percent. One of her hands was completely burnt off; the other was found with three fingers mostly intact. There were skin cells found under one of her remaining fingernails - the DNA came back to Alexandra West. Ruthie had a low CoHb level, as well as scarce soot in and around her mouth and nose. Her throat was bright red.

Jordon knew she'd have to review all of these findings tonight, before she re-considered the pathologist's testimony.

Meanwhile, the fire investigators concluded the fire was intentionally set at the foot of Ruthie's bed, but they found was no forensic evidence to prove who the arsonist was.

Jordon was sure the defense would argue her fire investigators were incompetent and the fire was accidentally set, or someone else was to blame.

The rental van was never found.

Jordon's phone rang again.

6

Friday, April 3, 2006 9:04 p.m.

Elder Abuse – Every person who, under circumstances or conditions likely to produce great bodily harm or death, willfully, or as a result of criminal negligence, causes an elder adult to be injured.

"Hello?"

"I think I'm on to something!"

Jordon loved the sound of his voice, especially when he was both excited and self-congratulatory. "What?"

"Not what - who! She's a woman our Evil Niece worked with."

"What? Where?" Now Jordon was beginning to get energized. She knew he wouldn't have used their slang term, Evil Niece, unless he was feeling pretty cocky.

"You're going to love this," he answered "at a senior citizen home in Wichita."

"What? We didn't know anything about any *senior citizen home in Wichita.* Where the hell did that come from?"

"Wichita's ABC affiliate KWAY." He responded, answering only the question asked.

"Okay, I get it. I'll shut up and you talk to me."

Jordon knew as long as she kept peppering him with questions he'd just slowly dole out the good stuff. She had to give him free rein or suffer the consequences.

"Okay, now hang in there," his excitement was escalating, "this is truly amazing. It seems that the story of our case and the hung jury made its way to the ABC nightly news last night. It must have been a slow news day and a woman being charged with an arson murder, well, I guess that's still pretty rare. Anyway, as I was saying, ABC's local affiliate in Wichita is KWAY. It seems one of KWAY's renowned call-in-viewers is a man named Bryan Swain. Apparently our man Bryan saw the story on the nightly news and then called KWAY to say he had some information for us."

The little inconsequential details, Jordon thought, are killing me and he knows it.

"Well, anyhow, it turns out an intern working at KWAY took Bryan seriously and called ABC's affiliate in Santa Barbara, KEYT. That intern then spoke to one of KEYT's interns who mentioned the call to Darcy Danielson - KEYT's nightly news anchor. Darcy's no slouch; she jumped on it and called S.B.P.D's Public Relations Officer, Pete McLafferty. Once Darcy secured an exclusive from McLafferty, should anything come of it, she gave him Bryan's Wichita telephone number. McLafferty then passed on Bryan's number to me. When I spoke to Bryan he told me he'd once gone on a double-date with the woman he saw on TV, and the person who set them up was Bryan's friend Doreen–"

"Doreen?" Jordon interrupted. "Oh my God – that's the name of the person who spoke to West on the taped jail call you listened to. Doreen is the one who said something about a 'Sylvia thing.'"

"D.A. Danner, shall I," Jake asked with sustained sarcasm "continue?"

"Yes, please, Agent Manchester." Jordon exhaled and waited; she already felt she was being overindulgent of Jake's torturously detailed narrative.

"Anyway," Jake continued, "Bryan recognized his date as the woman he'd seen that night on the news, only the name she used back then was Amelia Weeks, not Alexandra West. Bryan said he'd only gone out with her once because he thought, and I quote, 'She was really weird!' A few months after their date, Bryan ran into his friend Doreen, who gave him, and I quote, 'An earful of some pretty scary shit that she had later learned about Amelia,' A.K.A. our gal Alexandra."

"So," try as she might, Jordon could not contain herself, "do we know how to reach Doreen? Can we get her number from the jail? Do we know anything more about this Sylvia thing?"

"No, no and no. But before you interrupt me again, let me tell you that Bryan is, as we speak, trying to track down Doreen–"

"But he won't–" Jordon interrupted.

"Tip her off?" Jake finished her question. "No, it seems Bryan is now in the Wichita Police Academy and would love nothing more than to help us win this case. He's just going to run *intel* for us."

"Did he know the name of the Home?"

"No."

Jordon could hear irritation creeping into Jake's voice, but she was unstoppable. "Well," Jordon decided to go ahead and ask the theoretical question, "how many damn senior citizen homes can there be in Wichita?"

"Forty three," Jake answered "and that's counting the surrounding areas."

"Ahh, so you've already looked into that." Jordon was embarrassed. She should have known Jake would be all over whatever new information came his way. Their case couldn't have been in better hands.

"So you just called me." Her voice began to soften.

"To keep you posted," he offered, "share my excitement, and because I promised I would. So, how are things going on your end?"

Jordon never meant to, but still she continued to underestimate him, and most other people as well. "Nothing new," she answered. "I'm just looking over reports hoping I either missed something, or I can figure out another way to prove it to the jury."

"Well, I doubt you missed anything, but hindsight's twenty-twenty so maybe you'll find some nuance that could help you present the evidence in a slightly different way. But that of course is your area of expertise; my job is just to get you more evidence to run with. So, forge ahead, Bugliosi."

Jordon loved when he called her that particular nickname. She'd always admired the famous prosecutor and knew Vince Bugliosi had become successful by working hard; something Jordon knew she could do. "Hey, I miss you," she said. This time the words slipped out before she could stop herself.

"Well, than it's a good thing I've got my hands full down here because even you and a bevy of chipmunks couldn't keep me away. I'll call you back when I know something and then we'll see what's what. But in case I wasn't clear - I miss you, too. Bye, for now."

***

Jake chastised himself for telling her he missed her and teasing her about coming up. There was no way he could go up there and keep his hands off her.

He wished he could rewind the figurative tape of their relationship. He wanted to see when he fell in love with her and edit that part out. Men who fell in love with other men's wives had always disgusted him, and now he was one of them.

***

As soon as Jordon hung up, she felt like an idiot. She grabbed Caesar and held on tight. How could she tell Jake she missed him? She had to stay strong for everyone's sake. She took a gulp of wine and went in search of the experts' testimonies. Thankfully, she had ordered the "dailies" in this case. Having the daily transcripts to review, along with her still fresh memory, was a real plus. She decided to start with the pathologist who'd preformed the autopsy, Dr. Francis Rhinehart.

Jordon had liked Dr. Rhinehart - at first. Dr. Rhinehart was young, animated, available for questions, and pro-law enforcement. But by the time Jordon really got to know him, she wanted to smack him.

Rhinehart was educated at Harvard Medical School and did his residency at Duke. Rhinehart seemed impressed by his credentials, as was almost everyone else who knew of them. The only exceptions appeared to be a few doctors who wondered why Rhinehart didn't continue on with his Harvard education. In time, Jordon assumed it was because Rhinehart had said something offensive to someone at Harvard, which ended up making Rhinehart's pretentious attitude transparent. Later, Jordon became confident in her hypothesis, when Rhinehart told her he'd allowed himself to be talked into coming to the, "*non-intellectually stimulating*, hick town of Santa Barbara," because of his love for windsurfing. Jordon had never heard anyone describe her adopted hometown that way.

Rhinehart was tall and trim with longish, chemically-enhanced blonde hair. Below his lower lip was a closely shaven, and perhaps even slightly oiled, dimple. Between his confidence and manicured good looks, Jordon thought he'd at least win over most of the female jurors; Jordon was wrong.

Within moments of his appearance, Rhinehart's real personality came through, requiring Jordon to play catch-up the rest of the time in order for him to be deemed even credible.

Jordon now retrieved the transcript of his testimony. She wanted to see if she could improve their joint perform-ance. As she picked up her yellow highlighter pen, she reflected on some of her thoughts and observations at the time.

***

Monday, October 9, 2005 8:40 a.m.

They were beginning their second week of the trial. Jordon thought by then the jury's main question would be:

Was Ruthie murdered or could she have just died in a fire that was accidentally set?

Dr. Francis Rhinehart walked into court looking like a cross between the star of Miami Vice and a VH1 host. He was wearing a perfectly pressed khaki colored linen suit and a light blue shirt and tie. The shirt was a shade lighter than his tie and a shade darker than his contacts. In his right ear, the ear facing the jury, Rhinehart wore a diamond stud earring; he did so in spite of Jordon having asked him not to. He also carried a copy of *Vanity Fair*. Appropriately titled, Jordon thought, as she called him to the stand, but probably not a good choice to bring to court.

As Dr. Rhinehart approached the front of the court-room, Jake left his seat next to Jordon, seemingly to greet their witness, but in reality, to take the magazine away.

When Jake returned to counsel table he casually leaned over. "So do you think *everyone* noticed the title, or just us trained observers?"

"I hope," Jordon said, "just us, because I think, as usual, you saved the day."

"I guess," he shrugged, "I was half expecting him to bring *G.Q.*"

"Oh, no," Jordon whispered, "that just wouldn't do, *that* magazine wouldn't be intellectually stimulating enough." They each smiled as she briefly turned her back to the jury, while the clerk finished swearing in Dr. Rhinehart.

As soon as the judge invited her to do so, Jordon approached the podium to begin direct examination. En route she was surprised to see that many of her colleagues, both prosecutors and defense attorneys, were there. They clearly wanted to see how the county's newest pathologist would perform. And perform he did. Before Jordon even had a chance to say "good morning," Rhinehart lifted his hand to stop her, in doing so he exposed his streaky-tanned forearm. My God, Jordon thought, he uses some kind of tan-in-a-bottle and he doesn't even apply it correctly. What the hell kind of doctor are they going to think he is?

After stopping Jordon, Rhinehart asked the bailiff for mineral water. The bailiff rolled her eyes and brought him a Styrofoam cup filled with tap water. Rhinehart sighed, sipped, and frowned. Jordon feared his little vignette cost her dearly. He not only looked like the Prima Donna he was, but he had also obviously annoyed the bailiff, which outraged Jordon.

Jordon felt bailiffs were an influential connection to the jury because they were the only ones who were permitted to have personal and informal contact with them. Over time, Jordon had learned that an angry, or even annoyed, bailiff could unwittingly control the outcome of a case.

Not a single question had been asked of Dr. Rhinehart and Jordon already felt disarmed. She decided to begin by trying to impress the jury with Rhinehart's credentials, while at the same time not pandering to his Prima Donna image. Soon, however, it became clear to her that this part of the examination wasn't going well. Screw it, she thought, I'd better jump into the evidence right now or I'll risk losing the jury all together.

"Dr. Rhinehart, what was Miss Gold's blood alcohol level at the time of her death?"

"Point one six."

"From where did you retrieve the victim's blood in order to determine her blood alcohol level?"

"From where?" He tried to furrow his obviously *botoxed* brow.

His effort almost made Jordon laugh. "Yes, where?" Jordon looked down at her notes in an attempt to suppress her still percolating giggle.

"I didn't test blood." Rhinehart answered, "I tested vitreous humor, which I recovered from behind the corpse's eyes."

Rhinehart's response infuriated Jordon. She had asked him not to use the word "corpse." She told him it made him sound like the grim reaper. Jordon wanted him instead to use the word "victim" or "Miss Gold." Apparently, Jordon thought, he decided to ignore that piece of advice, too. Jordon resented being surprised in the court-room, especially by her own witnesses.

"Why," she went on to ask, "is it important to obtain fluid from that part of the *victim's* body?"

"Because," he acted as if he was stating the obvious, "that is where, in circumstances like this, one can be confident that the tested bodily fluid is not contaminated, and therefore the blood-alcohol level reading is most accurate."

Jordon ignored his affect and continued. "And what does the term blood alcohol level mean?"

Rhinehart rolled his eyes in the direction of the jury. "It means," he answered, "the concentration of alcohol in the blood."

"And does blood normally have any alcohol in it?" Jordon had to solicit sometimes even the most obvious of responses, in order to ensure that every juror understood all of the evidence.

"Not unless you are one of those bums who hang out by the fig tree." Rhinehart smiled at Jordon, enjoying his own warped sense of humor. Jordon didn't smile back.

Ooh, she thought, we certainly didn't need him to of-fer that commentary. If anyone on the jury was a supporter of our homeless population, Rhinehart definitely alienated them with that sarcastic gem.

"Okay," Jordon moved on as quickly as she could, "so, is it fair to say, in general, most people have a blood alcohol level, or B.A.L, of zero unless they've consumed alcohol?"

"Yes, well that's true for all people, not just most."

Jordon finally figured out that Rhinehart needed to show off; therefore, she'd either have to give him the space to do so, or she'd be fighting him all the way. Deciding it always appeared tacky to fight with one's own witnesses, Jordon smiled and said, "Well, yes, Doctor, I apologize, I misspoke; thank you for correcting me."

"No problem." Rhinehart smirked and sat back. He finally looked comfortable, having now established who the Alpha Dog was.

"Doctor, have you ever testified in any drunk driving cases?"

"Well, only the fatalities; after all I *am* a pathologist."

Jordon gave him her most synthetic smile. "Yes, of course. Now, in how many of those cases have you testified?"

"At least four." Rhinehart looked proud.

Jordon wasn't impressed. She knew if the defense attorney objected, saying four cases didn't qualify him as an expert in any aspect of drunk driving, she'd have to agree. Luckily, there was no objection, so she continued, not sure whether Adler had a plan or was just temporarily distracted.

"Well, Doctor, do you happen to know what B.A. level is deemed illegal, as far as driving a vehicle is concerned?"

"Yes, that's .08, but I don't know that in my capacity as a physician. I know it because I received the same DMV card in the mail that all your jurors did."

Rhinehart looked over at the jury and, for the first time, smiled at them. Only two of the jurors smiled back. Many of the other jurors either looked away or began to fidget. Jordon decided to go on to more dramatic testimony and return to the significance of the victim's B.A.L. later.

"Doctor, please describe the condition of what used to be the victim's hands."

Jordon felt the jury stop fidgeting.

"Sure, her left hand was burnt off down to the wrist."

Jordon glanced at the jury; they were all focused on Rhinehart.

"What about her right hand?" she asked.

Dr. Rinehart nodded, "Ah, her right hand; all but three digits of her right hand had melted away."

"Of what significance is that to you as a coroner-pathologist?" Jordon asked.

"It suggests to me that the fire was extremely hot by the time it reached her hands."

Jordon thought it was time for high drama. She slowly walked over to the clerk's desk and retrieved a photograph. She placed it in front of the defense attorney, who in turn showed it to his client. Jordon noticed the jury was staring at West. West showed no emotion. Bad move, Jordon thought. West should have been instructed to look sad. Adler's defense was either that his client didn't do it or her aunt died in an accidental burn. By not reacting to the photograph, West looked heartless; just the way Jordon wanted her to appear. In an effort to let that observation stew with the jury, Jordon took an extra moment to turn on the overhead projector.

Next she placed an index card in front of the projector's lens. Finally, she walked the photo up to the witness stand. "Doctor, showing you what has been marked as Exhibit Forty-Three; can you tell me what this is?"

"Yes, this is a photograph," he said staring at the picture, "of what was left..." his voice softened, "of her right hand."

Even Rhinehart, Jordon thought, seemed saddened by the gruesomeness of the photograph. That should score us some points.

"Doctor; what, if any, evidence did you secure from..." Jordon decided to use his words, "what was left of her right hand?"

"Matt Stevens from the S.B.P.D. crime lab was able to get her fingerprint off one finger, and that helped us identify her, but first I took scrapings from beneath her fingernails and those were later sent to the D.O.J. crime lab."

"Were you present when Mr. Stevens secured the fingerprint?"

Jordon knew the upcoming testimony wasn't necessary, but since TV shows like "C.S.I." had become popular, jurors seemed to appreciate this sort of detail, and she always wanted to please her audience. Over the years, Jordon had learned she should treat trials as both a search for the truth as well as a performance.

"Yes," Dr. Rhinehart replied, "In fact, *I* supervised Matt Stevens."

Jordon groaned inwardly; Rhinehart, it's not always all about *you*. Outwardly, she requested, "Please tell the jury, Doctor, what you observed Mr. Stevens to do."

"First, Matt asked *my* opinion as to which finger had the most skin. After that, Matt grasped what was left of her hand with one of his hands. Then, with his other hand, Matt held her third finger down on an inkpad. This was followed by Matt rolling her finger from side to side on a clean white sheet of paper. Finally, I took over and used a scalpel to scrape under her remaining fingernails. Then I placed the contents of those scraping in a small brown envelope, which was sent to D.O.J."

"Doctor," she asked, "by D.O.J. are you referring to the Department of Justice Forensic Crime Lab?"

"None other."

"Thank you," she continued. "And have you had an opportunity to review and consider the Department of Justice findings?"

"I have."

"And, can you tell me what those findings were?"

"Object, hearsay." Adler announced. "No foundation."

Jordon was pleased the defense attorney objected. She knew she had a solid exception to the hearsay rule and she thought Adler's objection, would bring even more attention to Rhinehart's response.

"Your Honor," Jordon responded, "Dr. Rhinehart is an expert witness. Since he relied upon those results in forming his opinions and conclusions, they are admissible."

"Ms. Danner, if," the Judge replied, "you can establish that, then I will overrule the objection."

Jordon proceeded. "Dr. Rhinehart, did you rely upon D.O.J.'s analysis of the fingernail scrapings in writing your autopsy report?"

"Absolutely!"

"Mr. Adler," the judge declared, "your objection, is overruled."

"Doctor," Jordon smiled, "please tell us about D.O.J.'s findings, regarding the victim's fingernail scrapings."

"D.O.J found epithelial cells, skin cells, within the scrapings I procured from one of her fingernails. They then performed DNA tests on those cells. The results of those tests indicated that the major contributor was Miss Gold. And, at a trillion to one, the minor contributor came back to," Dr. Rhinehart turned to the jury and announced, "the defendant, Alexandra West."

Jordon glanced at the jury. The jury was glaring at the defendant, who appeared unperturbed. Adler must, Jordon decided, have a plausible explanation or West would look anxious. Regardless, I need to cement the jurors' fury.

Jordon rose and removed the index card from the lens of the overhead projector. The jury looked up at the brightly-lit blank screen. Several members squinted; Jordon left enough time for their eyes to adjust. She strolled over to the witness stand, took the photo from the ledge, and placed it on the projector's platform. "Showing the jury what has been marked as Exhibit Forty-Three, Doctor Rhinehart can you tell them what they're looking at?"

"That is what is left of *Miss Gold's* right hand."

Jordon stood silently and stared at a hand composed of only three fingers. But she didn't stay still for too long; she didn't want to be viewed as either manipulative or theatrical.

A moment later, Jordon returned the index card to its position in front of the lens and continued. "Doctor, did you also have an opportunity to study the victim's face?"

"What was left of it," he said without emotion. Jordon was, once again, disappointed by his choice of words. Too crude, she thought, and just when we were actually beginning to win them over. Still, best to keep going. "Doctor Rhinehart, please tell the jury what you noted, about Miss Gold's face that had forensic significance to you."

"There was scant soot on her nostrils, lips and tongue."

"Why is that significant?" Jordon asked.

"Well, that, mixed with the fact that she had a low CoHb level, and extreme redness at the back of her throat, suggests to me she didn't live long in the fire."

"Before you explain your hypothesis, can you tell the jury what CoHb is?

"It's carbon monoxide."

"Okay, now please explain to the jury why you concluded Miss Gold didn't live long in the fire based upon the fact that she had a low CoHb level and extreme redness at the back of her throat."

"First of all," Rhinehart offered, "when people breathe during a fire, even for a few minutes, we see a notable amount of soot on their nostrils, lips and tongue. Secondly, we expect to see a high CoHb level in their blood. Here the CoHb was quite low. Finally, the redness in the back of her throat is consistent with laryngospasm."

"What's that?"

"That's a very common mechanism of death; it's when someone is suddenly exposed to a great amount of heat and opens their mouth to breathe. What follows is that the back of their throat gets extremely hot, swells up and closes. Moments later, they die due to a lack of oxygen."

Okay, Jordon thought, that was nice and clear; time to move on to the significance of Ruthie's B.A.L. "Doctor, based upon Miss Gold's: B.A.L., weight, and stomach contents, as determined at the time of her autopsy, can you opine how intoxicated she was when she died?"

"Yes," he answered I'd say she was extremely intoxicated, perhaps even completely out of it, that is until she breathed in her first and last breath of extremely hot air."

"Could she," Jordon asked, "have been too intoxicated to know someone was setting fire to her bed?"

"Objection!" Adler rose. "Speculation! This *expert* has already opined that Miss West was 'completely out of it'; that's at least within the realm of his expertise. He should not be allowed to speculate as to what was occurring during that time?"

"The objection will be sustained. The jury is admonished to ignore Ms. Danner's last question and not to speculate as to what the answer might have been. Move on Ms. Danner."

Jordon looked over at the jury; they appeared as if they understood the point she was trying to make. They also looked like they needed a break, but the time was 11:50. The next thing Jordon planned to do was unveil the most upsetting photographs of all. She knew the judge expected her to keep going until noon, but she hated to ruin the jurors' lunch. Still, she didn't want to further insight the judge, so she decided to be contrite and seek his advice.

"Your Honor," she asked, "my next series of questions has to do with the photographs the Court has previously viewed; shall I move forward now or wait until after the lunch recess?"

Judge Ames appeared to know exactly which photos Jordon was about to introduce and instantly agreed that after lunch would be "more suitable."

***

Lunch for Jordon that day consisted of rushing over to the local high school. Earlier that month, she'd agreed to speak at a noon meeting of the student's mock trial team. Her son Anthony was the school's history teacher and several of his students were on the team. Their final competition was only days away. Going there was the last thing Jordon had time for, and the one thing she'd never miss. Jordon treasured Anthony's devotion to his students; she thought it was one of many of Anthony's endearing virtues.

Jordon arrived at the school a few minutes late, having stopped to pick up Anthony's favorite lunch – a Rudy's *carne asada burrito*, something she'd special-ordered for him early that morning. Moments after she put the burrito in her car the smell of sautéed steak, onions, tomatoes, and chiles surrounded her. By the time she parked, she wished she'd gotten herself one, too, instead of the protein bar she was now wolfing down.

As Jordon walked toward the classroom door, she was worried about her case, still hungry, and disappointed she was arriving late. The moment she opened the classroom door and saw Anthony's spirited smile, all of her angst evaporated.

7

Friday, April 3, 2006 11:00 p.m.

Adverse Party – A party to an action whose interests are opposite to the interests of another party to the action.

Now, sitting in her log home almost six months later, envisioning Anthony's smile, Jordon thought again about his brothers and her husband. They were all out on a boat during a storm; Jordon was worried. And still, she thought, no word from the Harbor Patrol. Maybe, she considered, someone left a message on her voicemail at work. Having decided it was both important to check her voicemail, and to move around a bit, Jordon got out of bed.

She soon fell down onto the soft carpet. Looking around, she saw her foot was caught in the twisted, extensive, phone cord. In an instant Brutus and Caesar came running. Brutus began to bark while Caesar licked Jordon's face.

Greg had repeatedly told her the cord was too long, but she'd disagreed. Jordon thought she needed it long in order to take the phone into the adjacent room during late-night calls from law enforcement. When Greg suggested they replace it with a cordless phone, Jordon refused, explaining it was essential for her to have a non-electric line near the bed in case of a midnight blackout. True to form, Greg never mentioned it again. Instead, he unobtrusively rewrapped the cord whenever she left it unraveled. Now, after freeing herself, Jordon tossed the cord aside.

Once upstairs, she picked up their cordless phone, walked into the living room, and called her voicemail.

As she looked out the living room's floor-to-ceiling window she noticed the clearing night sky and heard, "You have one new message." While she walked closer to the window in search of her favorite star, she pressed "1" to retrieve her message.

"Hey Jordon, Ted Ross, here. Sorry to hear about your hung jury."

Jordon's search stopped. Just hearing Ross's voice jarred her.

"I was wondering," he continued, "if you'd like to consider offering Mr. Cantera probation. You know these kind of rape cases are a bitch for the prosecution to prove, and I'm sure after spending the last five-and-a-half months in trial, you could use a break."

Yeah, right, she thought, like he thinks I'd believe for a moment he actually gives a damn about my burden of proof, or me. Jordon could hardly believe his gall. She wanted to hang up, but knew she had to keep listening.

"On the other hand," his recorded voice continued, "if you decide not to take a break and do decide to retry West you'll have to delay our case and that wouldn't be fair to either your victim or Mr. Cantera. So, listen, I'm going to make *you* an offer, which is only good through Monday morning. You reduce the charge to sexual battery and my client will plead, as long as you agree to probation and no additional jail time. Come Monday afternoon we're gearing up for trial and that offer comes off the table. So give me a call before noon on Monday, or I'll just assume you've turned the offer down. So, that's it for now. Have a nice weekend."

Ross' click was followed by a computerized voice announcing, "You have no new messages."

Jordon tossed the phone onto a nearby couch. "Oh, great," she said, rubbing her forehead and eyes, "now I suddenly have something else to deal with." Jordon had planned to work on the Cantera case this weekend, but not to consider an offer, or to decide upon one, by Monday. She was sure this rape case would be a tough one to try, but she was also confident Cantera was guilty. Jordon didn't want to plea bargain this case away. Still, she knew the evidence was very weak and Cantera's lawyer was right: she was exhausted. Beyond that, if she retried <u>West</u>, she'd have to delay <u>Cantera</u> or reassign it to someone else. Jordon was positive another D.A. wouldn't want this case; and, she knew the victim would feel betrayed if she handed it off.

"Later," she announced as she leaned her head back and closed her eyes. And why, she wondered, *haven't* I heard from the Harbor Patrol? Jordon walked back over to the window, looked around, and placated herself with the notion that they were only going to call *if* there were a problem. So, she decided, no news must be good news. Still, she wanted to be reassured, I'll give it another hour and then I'll bug them again.

Jordon was tempted to pour herself more wine, but instead returned to the <u>West</u> case and the afternoon session with the pathetic pathologist.

8

Tuesday, October 9, 2005 1:35 p.m.

California Evidence Code Section 352 – The court, in its discretion, may exclude evidence if its probative value is substantially outweighed by the probability that its admission will create substantial danger of undue prejudice.

"Showing you what has been marked as Exhibit Forty-Four; can you tell me what this is?"

"A photograph," Dr. Rhinehart reported, and just when Jordon began to grit her teeth thinking he might not go on, he added, "of Ruth Gold's face, er, after the fire."

"And this? Referring now to Exhibit Forty-Five."

"That's a photo of her tongue and the back of her throat, after both have been dissected, of course,"

"Your Honor," Jordon asked, "may I now enter these photos into evidence? I remind the Court Mr. Adler has only stipulated certain items can be moved directly into evidence, and these photos are not on that list."

"Oh yes, of course, now may I assume you want to show these photos to the jury with the overhead projector?"

"Yes, Your Honor."

"Well then," Judge Ames stated, "Exhibit Forty-Four and Five can be moved into evidence. Defense Counsel's objection is noted for the record." Judge Ames then turned toward the jury.

"Ladies and gentlemen, much of what was just said, was said as a matter of formality, stated only for the record. Please disregard it. However, you may recall you were all asked, before being seated on this jury, if you could look at graphic photographs and you all agreed you could. D.A. Danner is about to show you two such photos. Allow me to remind you, if any of you need a break, at any time, please let me know."

Jordon was pleased Adler had objected to the direct admission of these particular photos; she thought it made it clear to the jury that the defense attorney didn't want them to look at what they were about to see. Jordon was also glad the judge felt compelled to make the announcement he did; she felt it took some of the heat off of her for showing the upsetting photos.

When Jordon removed the index card from the front of the lens, Miss Gold's partially melted face appeared. Only traces of soot surrounded her mouth and nose. Someone gasped. Jordon wasn't sure if it was a trial observer or a juror. Because she feared the jury might resent her for showing them the picture, Jordon didn't ask the doctor any further questions about it. Instead, she just briefly left the heinous photograph up on the screen and was respectfully silent.

The photograph of the victim's dissected tongue and throat had to be handled differently because Jordon felt the evidentiary value of that obscure photograph wasn't as obvious. "Now showing the jury what has been marked as Exhibit Forty-Five." Jordon placed, and then re-adjusted, the photograph on the slick platform of the overhead projector. Suddenly displayed up on the screen was an enlarged 3-foot tongue. Next to it was another similarly sized chunk of flesh.

Dr. Rhinehart identified the first image as the victim's tongue and the second as her throat. Then he pointed out that the back of her tongue and the beginning of her throat, "...which is, in fact, the opening to her windpipe, are both the same color - a flaming red." This photo remained on the screen during Jordon's in-depth examination. Ten minutes into this questioning one of the jurors felt ill and the afternoon session was cancelled.

Once the jury was sent home, Phillip Adler renewed his objection to the prosecution's photographs. "Your Honor," he argued, "those photos clearly violate Evidence Code Section three-fifty-two, in that they are more prejudicial than they are probative, and that was made clear by the juror's response. The Court should now exclude any of the yet unseen autopsy photographs."

"Your Honor," Jordon stood up, "the Court has already ruled on this. One juror's reaction, if in fact it was a reaction to the photo, doesn't change the legal significance of the photographs. This is an arson-murder case; you warned the jury what they'd see, and they told you they could handle it. These photographs are relevant evidence. Upsetting? Yes! Unsettling? Certainly! But this is a criminal courtroom, engaged in the most serious criminal charge that exists. We *should* find the evidence both upsetting and unsettling, or we have no right to impose a life sentence without the possibility of parole."

Jordon sat down; confident she'd said it all, without overstating her case. The defense attorney didn't respond.

"My prior ruling stands." Judge Ames said. "The autopsy photos come in. I'll see everyone tomorrow."

***

Many judges would not have allowed the defense attorney to re-argue a prior ruling, but Judge Ames always remained open to listening. Jordon was, at times, frustrated by this aspect of his judicial performance, but she felt the appellate courts appreciated it. Thus, Jordon's guilty verdicts, in his courtroom, were always preserved.

***

The next day, Jordon introduced testimony she was confident would end up being Adler's best exculpatory evidence; this was the evidence she feared could raise a reasonable doubt. Jordon brought it up first hoping she could take some of the sting out of its impact.

While still on direct examination, Dr. Rhinehart testified that, with the exception of West's DNA being found under one of Miss Gold's remaining fingernails, there was no other biological evidence found that would suggest West was the murderer. Jordon knew having her expert disclose this information first would make it clear that she was "taking the high road" and wasn't "hiding the ball" - two trial practices she always admired and tried to employ.

After showing the jury the autopsy photos, Jordan ended her direct examination.

Philip Adler cross-examined Dr. Rhinehart for two hours. He spent fifteen minutes making it clear that the epithelial cells found under Ruthie's fingernail could have gotten there by Ruthie merely grabbing on to Ms. West, especially if Ruthie were intoxicated. Adler also made it apparent that if Ruthie was "out of it," as Dr. Rhinehart claimed, she also might have slept through the beginning of an accidental burn.

Adler spent the remaining hour and forty-five minutes continuing to expose Rhinehart for the egocentric, self-congratulatory person he was and, as far as Jordon was concerned, that alone could have a devastating effect on her case.

By the time Jordon finished her re-direct examination of Rhinehart, she was glad she'd called him at the beginning of her case-in-chief; by so doing, she hoped the jury would soon forget his personality, but remember his words. He did after all, give Jordon a few pearls, which she intended to display during her direct examination of Todd Peterson, and buff up for her closing argument.

***

Well, she now thought as she put down the transcript, she had made use of his pearls and still she failed to bring justice to Ruthie. Jordon reached over a pile of documents and grabbed a yellow legal pad. She wanted to make a list of all the evidence she hadn't used the first time with Rhinehart but could use a second time. After meticulously dividing her long yellow legal pad in half she stared at the blank page.

Moments later the phone rang. Ahh, she smiled, saved by the bell.

9

Friday, April 3, 11:57 p.m.

Intoxicating Agent – Any agent, that when so used in sufficient quantities, produces entire or partial intoxication.

"Hello?"

"JoJo!"

It took her a moment to figure out which of her two men it was, and when she did, she was in fact, disappointed. She wanted to hear Greg's voice and know he, and their boys, were safe.

"Hey, what's up?"

"I found Doreen!"

Jordon was astounded. Jake then told her Doreen still worked at a retirement home in Wichita and she'd be in at eight the next morning. Jake decided to take the red eye and see her personally. Jordon appreciated him going, primarily because he was working hard on their case; secondarily, because he'd be out of town, and therefore unavailable. After talking about his plans they discussed the information she'd reviewed and the call she received from Ross.

"Listen," Jake concluded, "you've got a lot on your plate. I'll be back tomorrow, how 'bout I drive straight up there, that way we can talk about whatever I found, what you've come up with, and *us*."

Jordon didn't respond.

"Jordon, I know what I want, so it's really up to you. Come Monday night I'm out of here, maybe for good or, maybe just until we start up again. Either way I think it's best for both of us if you make your call by Monday."

Jordon said she'd try, but couldn't make any promises. They ended their conversation with her asking him to stay safe.

As she hung up the phone, Jordon realized she now had two intoxicating *agents* to worry about – Jake, and whatever rendered Cantera's victim incapable of giving consent. She never thought of Jake as an intoxicating agent, but that's exactly what this A.T.F. agent had become. Well, she concluded, she wasn't ready to think about *that* yet, but she did need to spend some time on Cantera. Ted Ross was also expecting an answer by Monday.

Now that she was distracted by the Cantera case, Jordon decided to temporarily put West aside. She thought she'd start by reviewing the Cantera investigator's reports along with the videotaped interview. She was hoping *something* new would jump out at her. *Something* that would help her decide to either dump the case or to go forward. Jordon picked up her file and looked at the last notation. **"Prepare for trial."**

Suddenly all she could think about was the moment Cantera's victim, Diana, asked Jordon if she could describe the defendant. When Jordon said she couldn't, because it would contaminate Diana's testimony, Diana replied, "I understand; it's just that I always had an image of what the guy I'd lose my virginity to would look like, and I just wondered if I was even close."

Picturing Diana asking that question still saddened Jordon, especially because Cantera turned out to be so despicable.

10

Saturday, October 20, 2005 5:55 a.m.

Rape of an Intoxicated Person – Where an act of sexual intercourse occurs, whereby the alleged victim is prevented from resisting by any intoxicating agent, and this condition is known or reasonably should have been known by the accused.

Diana never expected the long anticipated night out with her college roommates would end in the emergency room. Her first memory was of a giant scissor being used to cut off her designer jeans; jeans which had, at some point, become filthy.

The worst part of all, Diana told the investigator, was that she had no memory of any events past midnight. By the time she was interviewed, she understood that the authorities thought she'd been sexually assaulted, and she knew she'd vomited and urinated all over herself. Diana just wished she could figure out where, when, but above all - who.

The beginning of the video showed Diana wearing a hospital gown, sitting perfectly still, staring silently at the strangers who surrounded her. Moments later, when she looked over at her once beloved new sweater, she broke down and cried.

***

Jordon paused the video to look through a collection of photographs and retrieve Diana's publicized TV bio. It was hard to believe the person Jordon just saw on her TV screen was the same person shown, and described, in the document she was now about to review.

Diana Johnson was glamorous, tall, and slender, part Swedish, part Italian. She was the youngest of three daughters and grew up attending private schools in San Francisco. She first came to Santa Barbara five years ago; four years later she graduated from Westmont College with high honors. While in college, she volunteered at Girls Inc. because she wanted to, as she noted, "help empower girls and teach them to be critical thinkers." Diana was now working as a producer on a San Francisco morning news show. Her afternoons and evenings were filled with on-going community outreach programs, one of which was devised by her. The project she created involved children and the elderly working together in a vegetable garden. A photograph showed Diana's beaming face alongside a wheel-chaired senior citizen and his gardening partner: six year-old Armando. All three of them surrounded a giant sunflower.

Jordon was told Diana was devoted to her job, community, family, and friends. Jordon also learned that because of Diana's character and beauty, she was on the fast track to becoming one of the show's youngest anchors.

Jordon pressed "PLAY," knowing what she was about to re-watch, and dreading it.

***

The lower hand corner of the screen displayed the date and time - "10-20-05 4:55 a.m."

After the nurse left the room, Diana continued weeping until the interviewing law enforcement officer walked in. At that moment, Diana looked nothing like the fresh-faced TV producer prominently displayed on her bio. She looked, and no doubt smelled, like a drunk.

"Where..." Diana asked trying to focus her red and swollen eyes on the young Sheriff's deputy, "have I been?"

"We're trying to figure that out now, Ma'am."

Diana looked around. "Well then where are my friends?"

The deputy briefly spoke into his shoulder-supported radio and then responded, "We're trying to piece that together, too. So far, you haven't even been able to tell us your friends' names."

Diana dropped her head into her hands and cried.

The deputy looked ill at ease. Jordon knew no class at the Academy ever prepared anyone for their first rape investigation. Still, this deputy didn't make things worse; he didn't touch Diana or pepper her with questions. He simply, respectfully, left the room and decided to leave the initial questioning to the doctor.

"What...what happened to me?" Diana asked no one, but her face told it all.

***

Jordon paused the tape. What anguish, she thought, Diana looks miserable, helpless, and completely confused. Jordon was captivated and sickened by the image on the TV screen. She stood up and walked closer. The jury has to see this, she concluded, as she marked down the time. This frame should be turned into a slide and displayed during my opening statement. This will help the jury feel Diana's pain on the night she was raped.

Jordon sat back down and looked at Diana's frozen face. The worst realization of this kid's life, Jordon thought, had actually been caught on videotape. Jordon once again pressed – "PLAY."

The tape only lasted five minutes. Diana was exhausted and could barely communicate events leading up to midnight. Jordon next reviewed her notes from her first meeting with Diana; it had occurred one week after the assault.

***

"Every morning," Diana told Jordon, "I wake up, and before I even open my eyes I know something is really wrong.

Then I try to remember what that something is, and I can't. It's a blank, a black hole, a faceless-imageless pain. Then I remember what I've been told: that some man did something to me, but I don't know what and I don't know who. Then I realize it could be any man. It could be the man behind me on a set of steps or the one I'm riding up with in an elevator. And I don't know if anyone saw me or watched us, so everyone is suspect, and I don't…I can't trust anyone anymore…and worst of all is I know it's all my fault for getting drunk."

Jordon stopped her there. "You got raped because you met up with a rapist. What we should *expect* from getting really drunk is a really bad hangover. You probably interacted with lots of guys at the party that night. You were obviously drunk, but only one man chose to rape you, and that's because he's a rapist. Sure, it would have been better if you hadn't drank so much, but who doesn't feel that way the morning after. Learn from that, but don't blame yourself for the sexual assault."

Diana didn't respond. For a moment she looked into Jordon's eyes, as if Diana were trying to make Jordon's convictions her own, but then Diana said she needed to go outside for a cigarette and Jordon knew she'd failed again.

Every sexual assault victim Jordon had ever met, which included not just those who engaged in "risky behavior" but also children as young as four and adults as old as eight-two, always blamed themselves for the assault. Jordon understood it was just their way of trying to regain some sort of control over the most helpless moment of their life, but still, their self-blame always broke Jordon's heart.

When Diana returned from smoking, Jordon suggested that she make an appointment to see a counselor. Diana shook her head and said she didn't want to talk about *it*; she just wanted to forget about *it*.

Jordon knew Diana could never forget about *it* but felt counseling would help her put *it* in perspective. Even so, Jordon sensed her well-meaning suggestion was untimely; Diana just wasn't ready.

***

Jordon was still committed to trying to convince Diana to see a counselor, whether they went to trial or not; which is precisely what Jordon needed to figure out.

Jordon knew getting a guilty verdict in this case could have a positive effect on Diana's healing process. Conversely, Jordon had also seen not guilty verdicts, or even hung juries, re-traumatize victims. Beyond that, it was well known throughout the legal community that a negative outcome on these kinds of cases had a trickle-down effect, resulting in other potential assailants believing if they preyed upon an intoxicated victim, they could get away with rape.

Jordon was convinced, now more than ever, that she'd have to go through all the evidence, critically, for Diana's sake, as well as for the rest of the community, and if Jordon didn't feel she could prove this defendant's guilt to the standard of "beyond a reasonable doubt," she'd have a duty to accept Ross' offer.

Well, she concluded, my weekend is certainly filling up. I've got to figure out whether to re-try <u>West</u>, try <u>Cantera</u>, and in all my free time sort out what the hell to do about Jake. One thing I know for sure: if I don't re-try <u>West</u>, and I don't make some sort of commitment to Jake, I'll never see him again, and that's too painful to imagine.

The ringing phone once again interrupted her spiraling thoughts.

11

Friday, April 3, 2006 11:45 p.m.

Panic/Anxiety Attack – A sudden surge of overwhelming fear: raging heartbeat, difficulty breathing, and lightheadness.

"Hello?"

"Mrs. Danner?"

Jordon could hear law enforcement radio sounds in the background. Under normal circumstances, she would've assumed it was just someone seeking her expertise. Immediately, she sensed this call was different. Most cops joked around with her at first, and they all called her Jordon. This call felt formal, and personal.

Jordon's mouth went dry. Her heart pounded. The parade of horribles began marching through her mind. Who, she thought, had been hurt? Injured? Killed?

"Yes?" she answered. Both dogs immediately came to her.

"This is Officer Page from the Coast Guard."

She felt as if she'd been punched in the chest.

"Your son George radioed in. He had some trouble with the boat, there was a leak. The boat took on water…"

Jordon wanted to scream. Officer Page was speaking way too slowly for her. Jordon stopped breathing.

"…a lot of water, but they are out of danger."

Jordon didn't believe they were out of danger. She took a small breath, but knew it sounded more like a wheeze. Brutus dropped his head into her lap.

"George," Officer Page continued, "found a small inlet on the west side of Santa Cruz Island and they're going to hunker down for the night."

Jordon finally found her voice and immediately interrupted Page, "Did he say where he was?"

"Yes, he described it perfectly."

"Then go get them!" Jordon took on the assertive attitude of a District Attorney, mixed with the growling overtones of a mother bear.

"That doesn't appear to be necessary."

"Why?" Jordon's voice cracked. She thought she should try to control her vocalization, but she couldn't. Brutus stood up and shook.

"Because," the Officer took a deep breath, "George said they were fine, and quite frankly, unless it is a life or death situation it would be too dangerous for us to send someone."

"I'll pay for it!"

"Mrs. Danner," Officer Page slowed his speech down as if he were choosing his words very carefully. "We all know you're the District Attorney of Santa Barbara County," some of the respectfulness in his voice had now been replaced by his own law-enforcement assertiveness, "and we all know you could pay for the rescue, but there is no need for a rescue, the boat's captain said."

"The boat's *captain* is a *boy*!"

"Ma'am, with all due respect, your son is not a boy, and according to your local harbor patrolman, he is a well respected sailor. I spoke to Patrolman Swenson personally and he said if George said they were fine, they are fine."

Jordon was getting extremely frustrated with this government employee. She was used to getting her way with law enforcement officers and she felt this one was being obstinate.

After a few seconds of tense silence, Jordon asked, in a somewhat conciliatory tone, "Well, are you still in radio contact with George?"

"No, but I can call him back up, and you can speak to him through me. Would you like to do that?"

"Yes...please."

"Okay hang on a minute."

The minute felt like an hour.

"Alright, Mrs. Danner, I've got him on the line. What do you want me to ask him?"

"Just tell him his mother says, 'Hey Bubba.'"

"Hey Bubba?" Page's voice sounded incredulous.

"Yes, Hey Bubba."

"Okay, Hey Bubba, it is - stand by for his response."

Once again the delay felt interminable.

"Mrs. Danner, are you still there?"

"Yes."

"Okay, well the Captain's reply was, 'Hey Bubba,' but then he said he had to go and he'd call me back later."

"But he said, 'Hey Bubba' first?"

"Yes."

Jordon exhaled. Caesar sat down next to her and leaned most of his torso into hers.

"Mrs. Danner, are you okay?"

"Yes," she answered, "and so is my family."

"Mind if I ask what that was all about?"

Jordon was choked up, but felt she owed an answer to the man she'd just tried to bully. "Well, it started when he was about three," Jordon said through a tight throat and now soft tears. "I'd take him on catamaran outings. He'd be strapped in, behind me. At times the outings would get rough or we'd hit some weather. One day, I said, 'Hey Bubba' as a way to check in on him while I worked the sail. When I did he belted out a 'Hey Bubba' right back at me. Then I knew he was fine. On other outings, when he wasn't fine, he'd reply, 'Home now!' So that became our secret code through life, in all sorts of situations, only we haven't had to use it for a while." Jordon's voice trailed off.

Page cleared his throat. "So, because he said 'Hey Bubba' and didn't say, 'Home now,' you're confident they're safe?"

"Yes, as foolish as it sounds, that's exactly right, so, that's it for now, but I trust you'll stay in touch with them and me?"

"Yes, you can count on that."

"Thank you Officer. I'll keep the phone close by all night. And I hope you have a safe evening."

"Thank you, Ma'am, you too."

"Please call me Jordon."

"Thank you, I will."

Jordon hung up the phone, but couldn't move. Although temporarily comforted, she was still worried. She stared at the boxes in front of her. There was nothing she could do for her sailors; she had to keep working for her victims. Work, for Jordon, had always been her great distracter.

Jordon now had two very important cases to make critical decisions about and she needed to it by the end of the weekend. In spite of the complexity and gravity of the situation, Jordon was confident she could handle it; it was what Jordon did.

She always took on challenging pursuits and put in whatever time she needed in order to feel good about her efforts. It was how she made it through night law school, a full time job, and raising four children. Success for Jordon hadn't come easily; she was never the smartest student in the class, but she was often amongst the hardest working. Throughout her life, Jordon fought to make up for her lack of innate intelligence with thoroughness and tenacity; and she had to do it one thoughtful step at a time.

Step one, she now thought, back to work.

Grabbing a stack of documents and her legal pad she returned to the <u>Cantera</u> case. She'd already reviewed some of the information the victim had to offer, now she'd have to consider what the other witnesses and the defendant had to say.

Stephanie Brofmann was Diana's best friend. Jordon took another look at the group photo taken the night of the assault. Stephanie was the one with auburn hair, blue eyes, and freckles. As Jordon flipped through her file, she concluded Stephanie was the epitome of a type of California girl. She had endless energy, boundless enthusiasm, and a dearth of substance.

Diana and Stephanie drove down from San Francisco together, with, as Diana later explained it, "Steph's favorite CDs blasting and Steph dancing in her seat most of the way."

Now as she removed the various reports from Stephanie's file, Jordon found herself getting angry at Stephanie. The D.A. in Jordon knew better than to blame Stephanie for Diana's rape, but the mother in Jordon couldn't help herself. If, as the bumper-sticker proclaims, "Friends don't let friends drive drunk" then how does one excuse Stephanie's nonfeasance?

12

Friday, October 19, 2005 3:00 p.m.

Nonfeasance – Nonperformance of some act which ought to be performed.

Steph and Di, as they referred to each other, were roommates their last year at Westmont College, a small private school located in the foothills of Santa Barbara. After graduation the two moved to San Francisco.

Stephanie was now a junior purchasing agent at Macy's and the two shared a small apartment near Powell Street. This trip back to Santa Barbara had been their major topic of conversation for weeks. They were going to finally see old friends they hadn't seen since graduation. The plan was to be carefree and to party hard. This was to be the first time in months either had gotten away from, what they considered to be, their stressful jobs.

After arriving at their friend Sara's apartment at 3 in the afternoon, they went to the harbor for a late lunch of "crunchy fish tacos and icy margaritas." By 3:30, the three of them were joined by several of their other friends. As soon as the others came, Diana ordered another pitcher of margaritas. By 4:15, Stephanie suggested they go for a walk, but Diana thought they should first do a "quick round of tequila shooters;" Stephanie agreed.

A few minutes into their walk, they decided to run. After a short sprint Diana ran into the ocean fully clothed. Sara told Stephanie she thought Diana's behavior was "a little bit weird," but Steph just smiled and said Diana had been working hard, not having a lot of fun, and needed to blow off some steam.

"Still no boyfriend, huh?" Sara asked.

"No, you know Di," Stephanie replied, "she's not going to waste her time dating or screwing around with just anyone. He has to be Mr. Perfect."

"You don't mean? No way! She's still a virgin?"

"Absolutely," Stephanie responded "and I'm sure she's the only drop dead gorgeous twenty-two-year-old virgin left in this state. She needs to get really drunk tonight, let loose and have some fun!"

"We both laughed then," Stephanie later reported to Jordon, "but hours later those same stupid comments made us cry."

According to Stephanie, after Diana's swim everyone returned to their hotel rooms, or friend's apartments, to shower and change. Just before sunset, they met at the Santa Barbara Mission Rose Garden for a group photograph. Stephanie said they wanted a photo where they were "surrounded by roses and lit by the glow of the setting sun."

***

Jordon picked up that photograph. She was glad she had it enlarged for trial. In it, each of the co-eds looked more beautiful than the one next to her, but Diana was the most beautiful of all. Tied around Diana's neck was a colorful, shimmering scarf. The scarf's assemblage of colors united Diana's faint lilac eye shadow with her glittering blue eyes.

The officers later retrieved that scarf in the sand near where Diana had been raped.

Jordon reached across her bed, foraged through the box, and pulled out a picture of the scarf. The photo had been taken in the crime lab. Jordon stared at it. She could imagine Sergeant Spinier, the lab supervisor, methodically laying out the square fabric on a sterile piece of white butcher paper. As competent as he is, Jordon thought, Spinier couldn't *sense* the jury appeal of what he held in his hand. After all, even though he's a hell of a forensic investigator, he's still a guy.

What Jordon saw, even in the photograph, was that the scarf had died. The lively fabric, which just hours before had adorned Diana's neck, lost all its luster. Jordon kept staring at the photo and wondering how it was possible for an inanimate object to look sad, but this one did.

Jordon decided if she went to trial, she'd enter the actual scarf into evidence and then wait while the jurors passed it around. Jordon wanted the jurors to feel Diana's loss, and was confident at least the women on the jury would.

Now saddened by her own reflections, but excited about the newly-decided upon trial tactic, Jordon returned the photo to the file box. She had to continue reading.

***

According to Stephanie, the group next went out to dinner at Harvey's. Harvey's was a legendary local restaurant, famous for serving large portions of mediocre food and potent drinks.

Everyone the deputies interviewed who'd been at Harvey's that night remembered them. Arty, the bartender, even recalled the name of the customer who instructed Arty to send two bottles of champagne over to their table: the customer's name was William.

After he sent the bottles over, William attempted to join the group, but was rebuffed by Stephanie. In response, Diana followed him as he retreated back to the bar. Once they were away from the others, Diana offered to pay him back for the champagne. William turned her down and seemed insulted.

The next day, Arty, advancing William as a possible suspect, went to the Sheriff's Station and took the night's receipts with him. Once there, he met with Detective Muratoto, who thanked Arty for his efforts but acknowledged William was not their perpetrator. Still, the receipts as well as Arty was able to give Detective Muratoto a more detailed description of what happened.

Arty told Muratoto that while at Harvey's, Diana had at least two glasses of champagne followed by a glass of chardonnay; the latter being served along with her tortilla soup. At about 10 o'clock Diana asked Arty to call them a cab to take them to Isla Vista.

***

Jordon thought of Isla Vista, or "I.V.," as a blight on the county. Although it was the bedroom community adjacent to University of California at Santa Barbara, she felt it lacked the University's integrity. She often described it to her colleagues as, "One square mile of trouble, sandwiched between the mountains and the coast. By day, most of its 15,000 residents were docile, hard-working students but, each night several of its inhabitants metamorphosed into dangerous party animals."

***

According to Stephanie, the cab dropped their group off in I.V., near a house on the cliffs, which overlooked the beach. As soon as they got out of the car, several men yelled from the adjacent balcony; they were inviting the group up for a drink. The drink the men were touting bore the unfortunate name of "Sex on the Beach." Stephanie and friends reportedly ran up the neighboring steps giggling with anticipation. That was the last time Stephanie saw Diana that night, and until the next day, Stephanie never gave that a second thought.

Jordon learned from Diana that at approximately 11 o'clock, some of them decided to leave the first party and go off to another. Once there, Diana recognized the bartender, Sally Benson. Sally was another one of their old friends. At first, Diana thought this party was uncomfortably crowded, but as soon as Sally saw them she parted the crowd. In a flash, the room was pierced with shrieks of joy, immediately followed by hugs and kisses.

Several partygoers remembered their dramatic entrance and how happy they all seemed to be to see each other.

Diana stayed at the make-shift bar where Sally fixed her a double gin and tonic. Diana took a few sips at the bar, but when she became worried about taking up too much of Sally's time, she put her drink down on a table and headed for the dance floor.

Sally was the last friend Diana saw that night. Sally's only statement was, "Diana seemed fine when I saw her; otherwise it would have been un-cool for me to make her a drink."

Putting down *that* drink was the last thing Diana remembers, until hours later when she woke up at Cottage Hospital.

***

At first, Jordon thought someone could have spiked Diana's drink with a "date-rape" drug, but later when her urine was tested, it was determined no such drug was detectable, although it could have dissipated by the time the test was done. Regardless, Jordon knew the most frequently used "date-rape" drug was still alcohol and Diana had plenty of that in her system.

***

Diana's friend Cindy told the police she danced with Diana for a little while but soon lost track of her in the crowd. Sara reported she stayed at the bar when Diana went off to dance. Noreen told Jordon she'd been picked up at midnight by her boyfriend and felt too "wasted" to say good night to anyone. When interviewed, the other five girls last remembered Diana entering the second party and getting really excited when she saw Sally.

All of Diana's friends, when questioned, felt responsible. Jordon knew there was only one responsible individual, and by the time the cops found him he was very busy claiming, "She was all over me! Why don't you charge her with rape?"

Jordon decided she'd next consider the videotaped interview of Dan, the R.P.

13

Saturday, October 20, 2005 12:05 a.m.

R.P. – Reporting party; one who reports a crime.

Dan Pierson, like several of his neighbors, had attended U.C.S.B. in the early 1970s and never left I.V. Some stayed on as graduate fellows and ultimately became professors. Others bought small, boutique, mostly surf-oriented businesses. Dan Pierson fit into yet a third category; he stayed, but never evolved into anything. Instead he chose to spend his days sitting on the beach, smoking marijuana, and pontificating about "the Establishment." Dan's usual audience was a wide-eyed wealthy co-ed.

Sometime in the late 1970s, Dan's absentee landlord decided it was easier to make Dan the apartment complex manager than to chase him down for the monthly rent check. Dan recognized a good deal when he heard one; he needed to stay in I.V. By then he'd become completely dependant upon the adoration of young beautiful people.

Meanwhile, the University of California Police Department had been keeping track of Dan for years. His file contained misdemeanor arrests reports, booking photos, and notations of calls he'd made reporting crimes.

As Jordon compared Dan's recent picture to his old booking photos, she saw that Dan barely resembled the young anti-war demonstrator of his youth. Although he still wore his long tresses in a pony tail, his hair had become thin, wiry and grey. Over the years, his once taut bronze skin had taken on an orange hue, making the permanently puffy bags under his eyes look like small apricots. It seemed to Jordon, Dan's internal changes were just as significant; these days he appeared to spend less time questioning authority and more time worrying about his own personal safety.

Jordon pressed "PLAY."

***

"It was around one in the morning," Dan began, "I was dead asleep. All of a sudden I heard, 'No, stop! It wasn't very loud. Matter of fact it was so quiet I almost thought I must've dreamed it, but then I heard it again and it sounded like it was coming from the beach just below my deck. This time I could tell the voice was a chick's and she sounded real scared so I grabbed my sweats and got up. I guess I was a little freaked out 'cause I grabbed a kitchen knife and then ran down the steps to the beach."

Once he "hit the sand," Dan reported, he "carefully crept" behind the cement stairway. As soon as he peered around the column, he saw, "through migrating moon shadows," two human forms. Dan stood still and stared. Slowly it became clear to him that one person, a guy, was on top of someone else. Dan kept watching. A moment later, he was confident that the figure on top was a man and underneath him was a motionless woman. Dan took a step forward and "gasped." The woman's body was "all twisted up;" he thought she might be dead.

Dan assumed his "gasp" must have alerted the man, who quickly looked around and yanked up his pants. Then he lifted the woman's "mostly-limp" body and adjusted her clothes. In an instant, Dan could tell she wasn't dead.

"Still," he offered, "it was really creepy. They were both pretty messed up, but the guy looked like he was moving her around like a puppet. And even though I could tell they weren't going anywhere fast, I still ran back up to my house to call you guys."

***

The phone rang. Jordon felt disoriented. She pressed "STOP;" looked over at the clock and saw it was close to 2.

"Hello?"

"Hey gorgeous," She felt Jake's voice before she heard his words. "I assumed," he continued, "you'd still be up." Jake momentarily took her breath away; no man had ever had that effect on her. Come on Danner, she thought, answer the damn question. "Yep, wide awake. You?"

"Well, I'd better be. I'm about to get on a plane. So, how's it going?"

That, she could answer. "I'm actually working on Cantera at the moment."

"Boy, that's a sad one. How's the victim doing?"

"She's still walking-wounded. This dirt bag really did a number on her."

"I'm sorry to hear that. So, are you going to be able to put him away?"

"I'm not sure. Juries hate these kind of rapes. They always feel the victim is at least partly to blame either because she got drunk, or she wanted it at the time and later regretted that decision."

"Yeah, the old 'Monday-morning-quarter-backing' bullshit defense, but you know, there is such a thing as a false rape report—"

Jordon cut him off. "Which happens a small percentage of the time, just like all other false police reports." Jordon was suddenly feeling defensive; she expected that kind of nonsense from others, but not from him.

"Hey, I'm sorry. I know your case is legit, or you wouldn't have filed it. I've never handled sex crimes, not sure I have the stomach for it. Quite frankly, I don't know how you can do those kinds of cases. Give me a dead body and an arson anytime, over a live victim still living with the nightmare. Don't these cases ever get to you?"

"They get to me all the time, which is why I keep doing them. If it were your mom, wouldn't you want the D.A. to actually give a damn, rather than to just be going through the motions?" Jordon could hear herself sounding somewhat antagonistic.

"Yes!" he answered. "And there is no D.A. better than you! Remember me? I'm the guy who thinks you can leap tall buildings in a single bound. Hey, my plane's boarding. I'll call you when I arrive. I'd say don't work too hard, but I know I'd be wasting my breath. Just please take care of yourself."

Familiar words, she thought. "I will," she offered. "You too. Sorry I snapped at you, I guess I'm just beat."

"*Part* of what I love about you is your passion."

Jordon felt a slight twinge between her legs hearing him use *those* words.

"Still," he continued, "how 'bout a nap?"

A nap with Jake would be heaven, she thought…his warmth, his smell, and his muscles…

"Jordan, you're not falling asleep on me now, are you?" I wish I were, she thought. "No," she said, "but I think I'll take your advice. Have a good flight. Bye, for now."

Jordon quickly hung up; she was afraid of what she might say next. Sitting crossed-legged on the bed, she rubbed her face, stared at the pale phone with the long cord, and concluded I'm just exhausted.

Jordon turned the VCR and TV off, then pushed the boxes and tray of barely eaten food aside. Next, she puffed up a pillow and let her head drop upon it. The deflating cushion created a waft of Greg's scent. Feeling guilty and confused, Jordon closed her eyes.

Seconds later, she was falling asleep. As she drifted off she pictured herself on an aircraft, but as she turned to look at the man next to her, she fell into a deeper sleep before she could see his face.

***

Saturday April 4, 2006 6:00 a.m.

Jordon's alarm sounded. She threw the blanket off and sat up too quickly. Cold and confused, she looked over at the clock - it was 6 a.m. She'd been asleep for about four hours. She lay back down and re-wrapped herself in the down comforter. Moments later, having concluded she couldn't afford to waste any more time by sleeping, she went upstairs. While waiting for the coffee to brew, she decided to light the potbelly stove.

The stove had been recently renovated to burn pellets instead of wood. Jordon placed a few pellets in the stove's dish and then added some paraffin soaked wood chips. Next, she lit the small mixture and turned on the blower. Within moments of regulating the air she added more pellets. Not bad, she thought, for a nice Jewish girl from New York.

Soon the room was warming up and the kitchen smelled faintly of smoke, but mostly of dark roast coffee. Jordon was still tired. The old couch in the corner was beckoning but, she resisted its allure and went downstairs to get more of the Cantera file. She wanted to re-read the first responder's report.

Deputy Tom Evans was the first to respond to Dan's 911 call.

Jordon had known Tom for years. When she first met him, she thought he looked a lot like Ron Howard, the actor-turned-director. After working a few cases with him she decided he also brought a sort of "Ron Howard" sensibility and openness to each call he went on.

When Evans' report first arrived on Jordon's desk, she smiled and gave him a quick call. She wanted to incorporate his impression of the victim along with his carefully crafted words. Experience had taught Jordon these kinds of cases would rise and fall on the victim's credibility; a credibility she needed to establish.

Evans told Jordon he arrived three minutes after he'd been dispatched.

14

Saturday, October 20, 2005 12:18 a.m.

California Penal Code Section 647 (f) – It is unlawful to be found in any public place while under the influence of any intoxicating agent.

As Deputy Evans approached the beach, he was expecting to find a rowdy couple having sex. When he first saw them, it looked as if the female were hanging on the male, but as he got closer, he realized the female was so incapacitated, the male was actually holding her up. Now he feared the female might have been too intoxicated to give legal consent for sex, so, he called for backup.

The Dispatcher responded that Deputy Morningstar's E.T.A would be five minutes.

Evans then contacted the couple, identified himself and separated them. First he sat the female down and leaned her up against the bottom cement step, but as he propped her up, she began to groan. Most of what she said was incoherent, except for the words "no" and "stop." When Evans looked up, he saw the male's demeanor had changed; at first he was passive and compliant, but once the female began mumbling, he began pacing, and demanding to leave.

Deputy Evans told him he was "not free to leave, and was being detained for a potential '647(f) violation,'" though, at the time, Evans felt a much more serious crime had likely occurred.

Off in the distance, Evans could see Morningstar's patrol car approaching.

Evans knew Morningstar well, having been his field training officer after he'd graduated from the police academy, just nine short months ago.

***

Deputy Tim Morningstar finished an unsatisfactory 2nd in his class of 147. He was disappointed because he always strove to be the best. As far as he was concerned, he was born to be a cop, though most of the women in Jordon's office thought Tim should have been a model. Tim had no interest in modeling; he came from a long line of warriors, and more than anything else, he wanted to make his Native American elders proud. Jordon admired Tim's sense of justice, along with his golden-brown skin, black hair, chocolate eyes, and high cheekbones. Jordon's secretary, Kathy, once confessed she could barely remember anything Morningstar told her in person, because she couldn't take her eyes off his lips; lips Kathy described as, "deep crimson, sculptured, and thick."

Jordon guessed the only person who wasn't impressed with Morningstar's looks was Morningstar himself, who seemed to spend most of his free time helping his tribe.

Jordon felt Deputy Morningstar was a good cop destined for greatness, except for the fact that he'd run into some very bad luck on this case.

***

When Morningstar arrived, Evans told him to place the female in his patrol car and ask her the name of the man she was with; Evans doubted she'd know.

Morningstar helped Diana into his car. While belting her in, he posed Evans' question. In response, Diana looked bewildered, vomited, and fell asleep. The two Deputies briefly conferred and agreed Morningstar should take her to the hospital.

En route to the hospital, Diana began to mumble and Morningstar turned on his tape recorder. He wanted to capture Diana's slurred speech. The tape, he considered, might be useful as either evidence against her, in a 647(f) case, or as evidence against the guy if he'd done anything to her while she was intoxicated. Either way, Morningstar was sure his Sergeant would be impressed. They'd been issued the micro-tape recorders at "Briefing" just that morning and were told to use them whenever the situation warranted it.

***

Jordon clicked on the tape.

***

"No, no, no," Diana shouted. "Get urr hands off a meee! 'eave me alone!"

"Miss, what's your name?" Morningstar asked.

"Ya don give a fuck 'bout my name get urr 'ands off a meee."

"Miss, you are in a police car."

"Help! 'elp! *Po-liceman* raping meee"

"Ma'am," Morningstar began to sound unnerved. "Ma'am, I'm not touching you. I'm in the front seat, you're in the back."

"Help! Someone! He won't stop 'ouching mee."

For the next minute, she cried and occasionally yelled. Then there was silence; followed by the sound of the tape machine being clicked off.

***

Jordon pressed down hard on the "EJECT" button. The defense attorney, she thought, will have a heyday with this tape. After exhaling deeply, she returned to the reports.

***

By the time Diana and Deputy Morningstar reached the hospital, Diana was once again sleeping and Deputy Cummings was waiting.

***

Sean Cummings, like his long-time friend Tim Morningstar, was a new recruit and still on probation.   While in high school, Tim and Sean played football together.   Tim was a thoughtful quarterback, whereas Sean was an aggressive guard.   Sean's commitment to winning gave him the erroneous reputation of being callous. Senior year, Sean had broken his collarbone in a game, and his nose in the fight afterward.   Neither healed well, which only added to his falsely, macho image.

***

Once Cummings saw how helpless Diana appeared, he decided to forego the wheel chair and carry her into the ER.

After laying her down on a bed, he stood by like a loyal friend until the nurse shooed him away. As soon as he took a step back, Morningstar pulled him aside.

At that moment, unknown to both, Cummings also had his pocket tape recorder on.

***

Jordon played Cummings' tape.

***

"Hey, Dude," Morningstar is heard whispering, "you have to listen to this."

Morningstar then played his tape of Diana's cries for help.

After hearing the tape, Cummings asked, "What happened?

"What do you mean, 'what happened'?" Morningstar responded. "She was just going off in the back seat. She was probably thinking about what that piece of shit back there did to her, and I recorded it."

"You're fucked!" Sean announced.

"*I'm* fucked? Why?" Tim asked.

"Because it sounds like you were all over her."

"Me? Oh, bullshit! Here, listen again."

They played the tape again.

"Shit," Tim concluded, "that *is* what it sounds like. I *am* fucked"

"What are you going to do?"

"I got no choice, its evidence; I've got to turn it in."

"Yeah, ever since this morning's briefing, I've been using mine on and off all night...Oh shit!" Cummings tapped his pocket and discovered his tape recorder had been on too. "Well," he concluded, "now The Brass will have two tapes to listen to."

After that, Cummings' tape stopped.

***

Jordon later learned as soon as they returned to the station, Cummings and Morningstar gave their tapes, along with an explanation, to their Sergeant.

Sergeant Ensen listened to their explanation and told them to write a follow-up report. Once they left his office, Ensen listened to both tapes.

Ensen concluded Morningstar was in an untenable position, unless they got the suspect to cop out, or the victim, when sober, to say it wasn't Morningstar. Ensen picked up his phone, called the Detective Bureau and told Detective Muratoto to get the suspect's statements as soon as possible. "Then," Ensen added, "after the victim sobers up, get as much of a description of the guy as you can. I need this handled carefully and quickly. It's not just a matter of clearing a case," Ensen cautioned him, "it's also a matter of clearing a good cop."

15

Saturday April 4, 2006 7:00 a.m.

"Felony Ugly" – An in-house expression used by some prosecutors to describe a defendant who fits the stereotype of a perpetrator of the crime for which he is charged.

Jordon's phone rang again. She hoped it was news about her family, but when she heard Jake's voice she wasn't disappointed. He just wanted her to know he'd arrived, was going to grab some coffee, and then stake out Doreen's place of employment.

"So are you going to get a donut, too?"

"What is it with you lawyers? Actually, I am going to get a bagel - less sugar more class. Satisfied?"

"Actually I'd rather you had a full breakfast of egg whites and vegetables."

"Oh, yeah, that's real big in Wichita. Should I also put a sign on my car 'Police Officer – Undercover Investigation?'"

"Oh, you don't think they'll already know that? You're six-foot four, half black, half white, with blue eyes and cop shoes."

"I don't wear cop shoes."

"Yes, you do; they even squeak." They both laughed. She loved teasing him and admired him all the more for his ability to laugh at himself. "So, go get your coffee and *whatever*. And, please call me right after your meeting with Our Darlin' Doreen. I'm dying to know what you turn up."

"Will do. So, how's the Cantera case comin?"

"I'm still worried the bad guy will get off and the good cop will never be cleared completely."

"You've got to have more faith in the jury."

"I'm a little low on jury faith at the moment, but I've got some pretty good statements from the *perp.*, and some other stuff which I should jump back into now. So, I gotta go. Please be careful." Jordon paused for a moment, not sure how to say what she knew she needed to say. Suddenly aware of the awkwardness her silence was creating, she began talking before she found her words. "And Jake, about us... I don't..."

"I understand," Jake interrupted, "you stay focused on Cantera. I'll stay focused on Doreen and we'll talk about the other stuff later. Bye, Love." Jake hung up.

Jordon hung on. "Bye, Love," she thought: two words. How can two words paralyze me? Back to work, she instructed herself. Jordon returned to the TV to watch the videotape of Cantera's interrogation.

The tape began. Jordon stared at 42 year-old Ernesto Cantera as he stared at a blank wall. Clearly, Cantera was oblivious to the fact that he was being videotaped. Talk about felony ugly, she thought, he looks just like the pig he is!

Cantera's unshaven face was bloated. His legs were folded and his arms were crossed. Draped over his protruding belly were filthy hands with fingernails that appeared to have been recently bitten down to the skin. Jordon looked into his eyes; they were red, but not from crying. Cantera looked tired and perhaps even a little bit bored

He's certainly not the person Diana dreamed of losing her virginity to; he looks more like someone who'd frighten her. How dare he? Jordon clenched her jaw as she imagined what it would be like for Diana to see Cantera for the first time; which could happen on the day she came to court to testify.

"I'll get you, you heartless bastard," Jordon scolded her TV monitor, "for Diana's sake and for all the others who could follow."

But if I try, she thought, and don't succeed, then all he'll learn is that he can get away with victimizing woman. I can't try this one, she concluded, unless I can win it.

Just then, Detective Muratoto appeared on her TV set.

The smart cops, Jordon thought, always start recording before they walk in; that way, they make it absolutely clear nothing was said or done behind closed doors. Jordon was glad to see Craig Muratoto on the case; she couldn't have asked to have a better interrogator.

Craig Muratoto had been born, raised, and trained in Hawaii. While his large girth slowed him down physically, he compensated by using his mind more efficiently. His fellow detectives called him Sumo-Columbo, and although they didn't want to depend upon him to chase down one of their suspects, once caught, they all wanted him to do the interrogation.

***

Saturday, October 20, 2005 1:20 a.m.

"Good morning, I'm Detective Muratoto. Do you need anything? Food? Water? Bathroom?"

"Nah, I'm okay," Cantera answered, while unfolding his legs, thereby depositing a roll of fat onto the plastic chair.

Detective Muratoto then told Cantera why he'd been arrested, gave him a *Miranda* warning, and asked if he wanted to waive his *Miranda* rights and tell his side of the story.

***

Muratoto's gracious manner, along with his offer to let detainees "tell their side of the story," often resulted in getting confessions from many of Muratoto's suspects. Even so, most of the time, most of them lied, for at least the first go around, and Cantera was no exception. While Cantera was busy spinning his yarn, Detective Muratoto leaned forward and listened.

***

"Hey, man," Cantera said, "I don't know why I'm being blamed for anything. I'm actually the guy who saved her ass. I heard her call out and came running. I came to help her and then the other dude, he ran away. My only mistake was sticking around until you guys showed up."

In response, Muratoto made a few inconsequential inquiries and comments. His intention appeared to be to get Cantera to commit himself to that particular lie. Once he did, Muratoto told Cantera about the eyewitness, but Muratoto only told Cantera what Dan had *seen.* When confronted with those details, Cantera squirmed in his seat and initially responded with a few, "No ways." Ultimately, he changed his story.

"Hey, man," Cantera offered, "alright, listen I'm sorry for bullshitting you. It's just that I was trying to protect the bitch. Ya see, she was coming on to me. It's like we were dancing and she started to put the moves on me." Cantera's eyes lit up as if he were enjoying his own fantasy. "And she actually said 'fuck me' to me and I thought well, why not. So now I just figured when you brought me in here it was 'cuz she got sober, knew she screwed up, and then blamed me. So I thought, what the fuck, I can cover her ass and say someone else raped her, but if it comes down to saying I raped her, man I'm not covering her ass that much. I mean we met at the party, we danced, she started rubbing up and down on me and then she said, 'Fuck me some-where.' You should arrest her for rape!"

Muratoto tilted his head. "So did she say, 'Fuck me' or 'Fuck me somewhere?'"

"She said 'Fuck.' Fuck, I don't know exactly what the fuck she said."

Cantera no longer looked bored, sleepy, or even arrogant; he just looked scared.

"So, you don't know what she said?"

"No man, I swear to God." Now Cantera started swaying in his seat; "I don't know *exactly* what she said."

"So," Muratoto quietly commented, "she could have said, 'No.'"

"No way!" Cantera sat up straight. "She definitely did not say 'No.'"

"But she could have said…" Muratoto asked in the same monotone, "Get the fuck off me?"

"No way, Man, she didn't say 'No' in any way, shape, or form. She told me she wanted me to fuck her."

"So, are you telling me she never said the word, 'No'?"

Cantera vigorously and repeatedly shook his head from side to side. Then, avoiding all eye contact with his interrogator, Cantera mumbled, as if he were trying to convince himself, "No way, Man, she wanted it."

"Okay Ernesto, I just want to be clear about this, so take your time answering my next question."

Detective Muratoto became visibly calmer as his suspect became obviously more upset. Muratoto now leaned in closer and put his hand on Cantera's knee.

Good move, Jordon thought, act like you're giving him every chance in the world to back out before he hangs himself.

"Now," Muratoto continued, "think back…the whole time you were *doing* her…"

Cantera's knee started bouncing. He shook his head no, before Muratoto could even finish asking his question.

Muratoto continued, "Did she ever use the word 'no'?"

Cantera uttered his denial one more time and then added. "Hey man," he now looked up at Muratoto, "ya gotta believe me."

***

Amazing, Jordon thought, Cantera actually had the chutzpa to look Muratoto in the eyes again.

***

"She," Cantera continued, "never said 'No.' She wanted it!"

"Okay," Muratoto replied. "I'll be right back. Sit tight." Muratoto stopped looking at his suspect.

"Where ya going, Man?" Cantera asked. "What's gonna happen? Are you releasing me?"

Craig didn't answer him; instead, he turned and walked out of the room.

As soon as the door shut, Cantera's demeanor changed. First he began rocking back and forth in his seat. Then he stood up and started pacing. At one point he unknowingly stopped near the hidden camera lens and began to massage his scalp. Just before Muratoto re-entered the room, Cantera sat back down and dropped his head into his now sweaty, grimy hands. "This," he muttered, "is fucked!"

Muratoto walked back into to the room with a tape recorder. Cantera looked up; concern was brewing in his eyes. "What's with the boom box?" Muratoto didn't answer, instead he played Dan's 911 call:

"It was around one in the morning," Dan began, "I was dead asleep. All of a sudden I heard, 'No, stop! It wasn't very loud. Matter of fact it was so quiet I almost thought I must've dreamed it, but then I heard it again and it sounded like it was coming from the beach just below my deck. This time I could tell the voice was a chick's and she sounded real scared."

Muratoto click the tape off, sat down, crossed his hefty legs, and waited.

Cantera dropped his face into his hands. When he looked back up, his eyes were red, this time from looming tears. "Hey man," he declared through his dry throat and sticky lips, "I don't wanna talk no more. I just wanna glass of water and a lawyer."

Muratoto smiled. "Okay *Man*, I'll take that as you invoking your *Miranda* rights." Muratoto uncrossed his legs, slapped his thighs and stood. "So now I'm gonna bring you that water and a phone."

After he gave Cantera a cup of water and a telephone, Muratoto turned the video camera off. Doubtlessly, Muratoto knew taping Cantera's call to his lawyer was both unethical and illegal.

After Cantera completed his call, the phone was taken away, and the taping continued.

Cantera was told to stand on a large piece of white butcher paper, strip naked, drop all of his clothes, step off the paper, and put on a jail jumpsuit.

They wanted to collect every piece of hair, dirt, and fiber his clothes contained.

The tape ended after Cantera had donned his jumpsuit and was escorted out of the room.

From his last appearance on camera, it was clear Cantera's mood had changed from deviant to defeated.

***

Jordon turned the TV off. Damn, she thought, Muratoto is good.

That was the third time Jordon had watched the tape. This last time had now inspired her to finally write the memo officially clearing Morningstar, and also, to give Muratoto a call. Jordon wanted to see if he'd come up with any new ideas.

16

Saturday, April 4, 2006 8:02 a.m.

Newly Discovered Evidence - Evidence that had heretofore not been found.

"Detective Muratoto."

"Good morning Craig. Jordon Danner here."

"Jordon Danner?" Craig bellowed. "A call from The D.A. so early on a Saturday morning? What's up?"

"Do you have a minute to talk about the <u>Cantera</u> case?"

"Sure."

Jordon told Craig about her phone call from Ross and the review she'd been doing. "So, listen Craig, I'm wondering if you've have any other ideas that might help us prove these charges?"

"No, sorry Jordon, I can't say I have, but I've got some time this morning, so why don't I do what you're doing - review the case and see if something new jumps out at me."

Jordon wasn't surprised Craig hadn't had any new ideas; she thought calling him was a long shot. Still, she was glad he offered to review his file. Jordon then gave him her telephone number and asked him to call if something significant came up.

***

Craig pulled out his file and put up his legs.

An hour later something caught his eye. He tugged his legs off the desk and reached for the phone.

***

Jordon looked up at the clock; it was nearing 9:00 a.m.

I've got just enough time, she thought, to go for a quick run before Jake calls.

Jordon dressed and went back upstairs. Her legs were aching both from stiffness and lack of sleep. After drinking a glass of water, she leaned on the kitchen counter and looked out a frosted window. Distant snow-crowned mountain tops reflected the morning sun. Jordon squinted, walked over to the back porch door, opened it, and took a deep breath. Wearing only a tee shirt and shorts, she stepped outside.

Seconds later, the revitalizing cool air felt just plain cold and Jordon retreated inside. After grabbing a sweat-shirt, gloves, and an old Green Bay Packers beanie, Jordon put on her earphones, connected the iPod, pulled down her cap, and left.

Five minutes into her run, she was already feeling better. The air smelled just like new snow. Another twenty minutes went by and she still hadn't passed another human being, although she had passed three bunnies, a doe, and her fawn. Further up the road, near the clubhouse, she spotted some morning golfers and tennis players. A few smiled and nodded, but no one tried to talk to her.

Jordon loved her mountain community. Those who bought second homes up here, like her, did so to get away from their stressful city jobs. Thankfully, in this community, there was a non-discussed but mutually agreed upon commitment that nobody would ask about the other's city life; still, if anyone wanted to talk about it themselves, there was always a sympathetic ear nearby.

Another thing Jordon appreciated about her alternate surroundings was the unspoken rule that city morays would not be applied arbitrarily. As Jordon ran up the trail, she sang out loud with Faith Hill, who was now belting out her version of Janis Joplin's famous song, "Take it – take another little piece of my heart." Jordon never felt inhibited about looking foolish in her mountain community: she wouldn't dare do what she was doing in S.B.: not very D.A.-

like, as her friend Deidre would say. Jordon smiled, as she thought of Deidre.

Deidre and Jordon had become best friends in law school. After graduation, Jordon soon realized what she liked best about going to law school was knowing she'd have a chance to talk to Deidre three times a week.

Damn, Jordon thought, I wish we could have one of our chats right now. I'd love to tell her about Jake. I know she wouldn't like hearing it, because she adores Greg, but I'm also sure she'd understand, and still love me despite my poor judgment.

"Take it - take another little piece..." Jordon continued to sing her duet with Faith as she now pulled her sweatshirt off: the day was warming up. After she tied the shirt around her waist, she began to sprint.

Moments later, with resentment of her aching middle-aged muscles, Jordon returned to her usual pace.

Once she realized she'd been away from her phone for almost an hour, her concern about all her boys intensified and she sprinted home.

***

Even before getting a drink of water, Jordon called the Coast Guard's telephone number. She then took the portable phone into the living room, and sat down on the old rocking chair. Looking up, she faced their mantle; it was lined with Greg's favorite antique bottles and glass.

Greg had been digging up old bottles and glass since he was a boy. Jordon had chosen those eight pieces, from the dozens he'd found, because the circumstances surrounding their excavations always made Greg feel proud.

Jordon grinned as she thought of the hours Greg spent holding the glass fragments up toward the sun and rotating them like kaleidoscopes.

"Hello? Hello? Is anyone there?"

"Good morning, Officer Page. My apologies; my mind was temporarily some place else. Tell me have you heard from my family yet this morning?"

"No Ma'am, I haven't, but I didn't expect to, either. You know I can call 'em up on the radio again, if you reckon it will make you feel better."

'Reckon it'll make me feel better,' she repeated to herself and smiled, I haven't heard an expression like that since I stopped watching *Bonanza* re-runs. Despite her better judgment, Jordon answered, "Yes, Officer, I reckon it would."

The phone went dead. Jordon didn't know if Page was offended by her use of his word, or if he was just doing what he offered to do. A moment later she got her answer.

"Ma'am, I got 'em on the other end. What do you want me to say? That Bubba thing again?" Page seemed serious and anxious to please.

"No, no thank you. Please just find out what's going on, if they need anything, and when they think they'll be back."

"Okay Ma'am, I'll be right back at you." Once again, the phone went dead, this time for several minutes. Soon Jordon began to imagine the worst.

"Okay Ma'am, I spoke to your husband. He said to tell you he loves you."

Jordon felt warmth, which was quickly overwhelmed by guilt.

"And he said that he and George were still working on fixing the boat, which they've just about got nailed. And Sam was still fishing for that calico bass. Mr. Danner also said he thought they'd be home Sunday night, but no earlier than 9 o'clock. Did I cover everything, Ma'am?"

Jordon smiled. "Yes. Thank you, Officer."

"You're welcome, Ma'am, but, do you want to say anything back?"

"Just tell them I love them..." she was silent for a moment as her throat constricted, "and Godspeed."

"Will do, Ma'am, over and out."

The phone went dead. They were all safe and they'd be home tomorrow. Jordon wasn't crazy about her sixteen-year-old spear fishing on his own, but she knew she had to 'lighten up.' After all, he was almost seventeen and his father and big brother were watching over him. Still, she thought, he was "the baby," and therefore ever vulnerable.

"Okay," she said out loud, "Back to work."

17

Saturday, April 4, 2006 9:15 a.m.

Obstruction of Justice – A volitional act which impedes a lawful investigation or order.

"Arty Lang?"

"Yes."

"This is Detective Muratoto from the Santa Barbara Sheriff's Department."

Arty's heart started galloping.

"Yeah, err, hi. What's up?" Arty's stomach began to ache.

"Well, Arty, I'm calling regarding the case you came to see me about."

"Un huh." Arty decided to say as little as possible.

"I was re-reading my notes from when we spoke."

"Un huh."

"And I began to wonder about something you said…"

***

Arty, Muratoto thought, sounds very uncomfortable.

"You told me, just when you were leaving my office, that you hoped you weren't going to get blamed for anything."

"I said that?"

"Yeah, it's right here in my notes. So I'm wondering what exactly did you mean by that?"

"What did I mean by that?"

Muratoto's suspicions always increased when his questions were repeated, instead of answered.

***

Stall, Arty thought, bullshit and stall.

"I, err, meant I didn't want to get in any trouble with you guys for serving someone who was kinda drunk."

"So you were worried about getting in trouble with us?"

Whoah, Arty thought, that sounds bad.

"Well," Arty answered, "not so much you but err, maybe my boss at Harvey's, you know, for serving her or maybe for bringing you guys the receipts without you getting a warrant or nothing."

"Yeah," Muratoto interrupted, "I was wondering about that. Why were you being so helpful?"

Arty now feared Muratoto was on to him. "Hey man, that's just the kind of guy I am."

***

"Well then, hey man," Muratoto concluded their conversation, "thanks. I'll be seeing you. Take care."

The line went dead.

After Muratoto hung up he walked over to his computer. Next, he sought Arty's D.M.V photograph and RAP sheet.

Muratoto thought the picture on Arty's license made him look like a skinny-dark-haired-beatnik. Muratoto then discovered Arty had only two entries on his RAP sheet. The first was a conviction for misdemeanor "trespassing/peeping." The second showed he'd applied for fingerprint clearance to substitute teach at a local photography school.

Hmm, thought Muratoto, so all I really know about this guy is that he's a bartender and a peeper who likes to take photographs.

18

Saturday, April 4, 2006 11:15 a.m.

Inculpatory Evidence – Evidence tending to show a person's involvement in a crime; incriminating evidence; the opposite of exculpatory evidence.

Cantera or West? Neither, she decided, and called Jake instead.

His cell phone rang once. "Where have you been?" he asked. "First the line was busy, then - no answer!"

"Good morning to you, too." Jordon replied.

"We said 'good morning' hours ago." He took some of the edge out of his voice. "So where have you been?"

Jordon didn't like explaining her actions to anyone. Resenting both his question and his tone, she didn't answer him.

"Jordon?"

"Yes?"

"I'm sorry… I didn't mean to sound like a possessive husband."

You can't, she thought, because you're not my husband and Greg would never ask me that question or use *that* tone of voice. Jordon surprised herself with her strong reaction; Jake's question wasn't unreasonable, it was just…

Jake continued, "It's just that I've been calling for a while and I know how much stress you've been under, and how little sleep you've had. I was worried about you."

Jordon didn't know what to say, he hadn't done anything wrong, but she was still put off.

"I'm also," Jake acknowledged, "running on empty myself, both physically and emotionally, and I suppose I just wanted to connect."

"Jake," Jordon finally spoke, "you know we're connected. I'm just struggling to figure out what that means. Anyway, I was out jogging and thank you for worrying about me." Why, Jordon wondered, did she have such a strong reaction to Jake describing himself as a possessive husband? I probably should give *that* some thought.

"Hey, I'm sorry," he offered, "it's just that you're always on my mind."

"Yeah, yours and apparently Willie Nelson's, too." Jordon smiled and sensed Jake did too; they both loved that song. "So," she continued, "what have you got? Did you see Doreen? Is she everything you'd hoped she'd be?"

"Oh, yes, everything and more!"

Jordon was taken aback. If he had big news about their case, how could he talk about his feelings toward her first? "Tell me everything," she asked, "but first tell me - the more."

Jake took a deep breath. "Well, it seems Doreen was involved in covering up a suspicious death at the Wichita Friendship Manor and *who* do you think that victim's caretaker was?"

"No shit! Our own dear Alexandra West?"

"None other, only she didn't use that name in those days. In those days she was known as Amelia Winters"

"Hot damn! Okay, now tell me the rest."

"I will, but under one condition - you don't interrupt me. Grab a pad and write down your questions. If, by the time I finish I haven't addressed them all, then you can fire away, okay?"

Jordon understood his proviso. She knew she had an annoying habit of interrupting people. She usually felt that it was the most efficient way for her to have a conversation, but when the other party was Jake, interrupting was a waste of time. Jordon reached over, grabbed a legal pad, and hoped she could contain herself.

"Ready!" She announced.

"It seems Amelia," Jake began, "again, as Alexandra was known in those days, worked in Wichita's Friendship

Manor as an aide. Apparently early on, Amelia developed a reputation for being a little 'rough' with the patients. Doreen opined, Friendship Manor kept Amelia on, in spite of her reputation, because filling the aide job with 'people who spoke English was tough.'

"At first, Doreen liked Amelia, because she 'wasn't mean to her like the other aides were.' Doreen, herself, is somewhat developmentally delayed, but I'll tell you more about that later. Anyway, beyond being nice to Doreen, Amelia also initially made her laugh, and together they'd 'make fun of the cranky patients.' Still, at some point Doreen thought Amelia's humor 'went too far.' Doreen said Amelia started 'messing with the patients' by feeding them too slowly or promising to take them outside for a walk, knowing full well she couldn't do that. On occasion, Doreen would see Amelia 'yell back at the mean patients and make them cry,' and although Doreen didn't feel too bad about Amelia doing that, what bothered her was how much Amelia seemed to enjoy watching those patients cry.

"Ultimately, Doreen found the courage to ask Amelia why she 'messed with the patients.' According to Doreen 'Amelia went nuts' and let her have it 'with both barrels.' Amelia told Doreen that all the patients were *'a bunch of old parasites who should die.'*"

Jordon could no longer contain herself. "Did Doreen say our girl actually used those words?"

"Yes," Jake answered, "and that's one."

"Okay," Jordon groveled, "I'm sorry, no more interruptions, I promise. Please go on. What did Doreen say after that?"

"That Amelia made it clear she'd had her fill of the 'old codgers.' At some point, Amelia told Doreen, she'd been raised by her Grandmother who apparently used to physically abuse her when she was a child, emotionally abuse her when she was a teenager, and throughout threatened her that if she left, she'd inherit nothing. Doreen said Amelia told her she stayed with this grandmother until the end, but still inherited nothing. Amelia also made it clear to

Doreen that Grandma was the reason she missed all the 'good stuff' in life, like marriage and 'even graduating from high school.' Doreen always thought Amelia seemed 'really pissed off' when she talked about her Grandmother, or for that matter, any of the patients at Friendship.

"As time went on, Doreen tried to distance herself from Amelia, but Amelia responded with threats, telling her if she ever heard that Doreen had 'ratted her out' to the bosses she'd tell them all the 'naughty' things Doreen had said. After being threatened, Doreen never spent any more time with Amelia, but she also didn't tell the administration about how Amelia treated the patients.

"Evidently, Doreen is considered a special employee because at some point she was diagnosed as mildly retarded, which, in Doreen's mind, made her barely employable, and not very credible. Still, Doreen worried 'all the time' about what Amelia would do. Which brings us to the murder cover up. Still with me?"

"Yes, go on."

"Okay, it seems that one evening Doreen saw Amelia go into a patient's room with a food tray. After Amelia walked into the room, she shut the door behind her; that seemed suspicious to Doreen, so she stood outside and listened. The patient's name was Sylvia. A few minutes later Doreen heard Sylvia 'coughing hard' so Doreen walked in. What she saw terrified her; Sylvia was turning blue and, 'Amelia was way over on the other side of the room, smiling.' Doreen screamed for help. Amelia glared at her, and then walked over to Sylvia's bedside. The nurses ran in, but by the time they arrived it was too late: Sylvia was dead."

"Oh, my God," Jordon cried out, "Alexandra's even more of a monster than I imagined. Why didn't the hospital nail her?"

"Because the investigation didn't prove any malfeasance on Amelia's part, but that's because Doreen never reported what she really saw. My guess is Friendship Manor was embarrassed by the whole incident, and rather than risk being sued by Sylvia's family, they didn't pursue a very thorough investigation. Instead, they likely accepted Amelia's resignation and agreed neither would mention the 'unfortunate' incident again.

"So, anyway, when Doreen saw Alexandra's picture on TV, along with the story about the hung jury, she recognized Alexandra as her old co-worker Amelia. After getting over the initial shock, Doreen called the Santa Barbara County jail and somehow left a message for Alexandra. It seems Doreen wanted to know if Alexandra was really Amelia. Well, Alexandra called her back - collect, and made it clear, in vague terms of course, that if Doreen called the cops now, she'd be in trouble.

"Doreen told me she wasn't so sure about that so, she *decided* to call the police in Santa Barbara, but suddenly I showed up, so she thought I was 'God-sent.' Okay Jordon I'm impressed, you only interrupted once - fire away."

"No fucking way!"

"And for that you wasted your parents' money on a fine law school education?"

"I paid my own way through law school, and I only use profanity when I am wowed, and you, my hero, have completely wowed me."

"Hmm, I guess I've been demoted. Just an hour ago I was 'God-sent,' now I'm merely a mortal hero. My fall from Grace cuts deep within my soul."

"Oh, you'll get over it, but for now I want you to make sure Doreen knows even though the statute of limitations has passed for her potential criminal culpability, she could still be sued or fired. Next, if she agrees, I'd like for someone to videotape you interviewing her. You need to get her to explain everything that happened, right from the beginning. After that come back with the video as well as Doreen's signed promise to appear. That is, if she still agrees to go forward–"

"Don't worry," Jake interrupted, "she'll sign the statement, agree to the videotaping, and appear. She wants to get this off her chest. After all, she did keep saying over and over again I was 'God-sent.' But just to keep her honest, I did audiotape my first interview of her, so, when she testifies, *if* you do need to impeach her with a *prior inconsistent statement*, you've got it. See, I am God-sent!"

Jordon laughed out loud, but inside she knew she couldn't disagree. Still, she had a few more questions. "What will a Santa Barbara jury think of Doreen?"

"Well, before they start to *think,* they'll *feel* sorry for her. She looks, and acts, somewhat slow. Beyond that she wears too much blue eye shadow, which is big in this part of Kansas, and she doesn't appear to be a careful dresser. Once the jury gets past all that surface stuff, they'll be angry at her for not going to the authorities sooner. But what I think is important here is that they'll probably believe her and gain some great insight into who Alexandra West really is."

Jordon thought Jake's analysis sounded about right. "Okay," she directed, "now we're also going to need to corroborate what she reported—"

"I'm all over that, too," he again interrupted. "I found Sylvia's death notice online in the local paper. And Doreen gave me a short list of names of people who worked at Friendship back then, and who she thinks might cooperate with us now. As we speak, I'm heading over to the Wichita A.T.F./F.B.I. office to see what they and the local authorities have on all this. After that, I'm looking to get a search warrant to get into Friendship's files - including Amelia's and Doreen's employee records, the so-called investigation reports, and info on Sylvia's family. However, I fully expect most of that stuff was destroyed a long time ago." Jake took a deep breath. "Finally, I'm going to try and see if I can find out anything about West's grandmother; I figure that could help you with the pattern/motive issue - proving up some sort of elder abuse. Anything else, counselor?"

"Okay, Big Shot, nothing else I can think of... at this moment. Damn, you're good."

"Like I've been telling you—"

Jordon interrupted his teasing sexual overtone, "So now we should be in great shape for Monday with all the new inculpatory evidence you've got."

"Not so fast, I still have another lead to follow up on. You know, the gardener, Ming."

"Oh, yeah," Jordon remembered, "so what do you think that's about?"

"I have no idea, but I'm on a roll. I'll spend the rest of today getting you your tape, and the ball rolling on the other stuff. If all goes well, I should be able to catch the red-eye back and spend Sunday tracking down Ming."

"Jake, you're amazing!"

"Yeah, yeah that's what I've been telling you," Jake replied, rekindling their old joke. "Wait until you see just how truly amazing I really am."

Jordon uncharacteristically blushed. Jake was clearly feeling good, she thought, even teetering on cocky. "Just get home safely," she said, "and call me when you do."

Jordon was relieved he was no longer talking about coming up to see her. He was obviously excited about this newly-discovered explosive evidence and was hungry for more.

"Will do," he replied.

Jordon could feel his smile from 2,000 miles away. She had to add one more thing: "Congratulations, Agent Manchester."

"Thank you District Attorney Danner, I'll call you later. Take care, Babe."

He hung up, and still she hung on, but only for a moment. His brilliant discovery clinched it: they'd re-try the case. Therefore, Jordon would have to re-consider their arson investigator's testimony.

19

Monday, November 4, 2005 8:00 a.m.

Arson Investigator – One who has the authority and responsibility to trace or track; to search into; to examine and inquire into, with care and accuracy, the cause and circumstances surrounding a fire.

Todd Peterson decided to arrive a half hour early. Once there, he sat down on his favorite rustic wooden bench - the bench located just outside the courtroom door. Todd used the time to mentally review his reports and to psych himself up. In spite of his apprehension, Todd loved to testify. He enjoyed both the mental gymnastics and, to a lesser extent, showing off. Todd worked long and hard for his flawless reputation and he wasn't about to let any skillful defense attorney trip him up.

When Jake stepped out of the courtroom to escort Todd in, Todd was leaning forward. The moment Jake nodded, Todd rose to his feet. They smiled, shook hands and walked in together. Todd was more than ready.

***

As Jake and Todd walked into court, side by side, Jordon was struck by their collective attractiveness and confidence.

Jordon watched the jurors as Todd approached the stand and sensed several of the female jurors wanted to believe him, even before he was sworn in. Still, as she'd learned from her recent experience with Dr. Rhinehart, Todd's sandy hair and deep brown eyes wouldn't be enough. But Todd's different, she thought, he has knowledge based upon hard work and experience. This jury is not only going to conclude he's credible, they'll also find his testimony riveting.

Unlike many who testified, Todd made the witness stand his own. He moved the chair up and the microphone down. Later, she learned he even found a small ledge, out of the jury's view, upon which to rest his feet. Once situated, Todd didn't touch his hair or his face. Nor did he, as did many nervous expert witnesses, shuffle or look through his notes; Todd couldn't do that, because he didn't bring any notes – he didn't need them. No one knew this fire scene better than he. Instead, Todd just placed his newly-shinned laser pen on the railing and his hands in his lap. When the bailiff offered Todd water, he declined, as Jordon knew he would. Todd treated testifying like a difficult mountain bike ride, which he in fact enjoyed every other day. In both cases, Todd always hydrated early and consumed nothing during the actual event.

Jordon stepped up to the podium and smiled; she couldn't wait to hear Todd testify. After he was sworn in, Jordon began by asking about his formal education; she knew this was Todd's Achilles Heel. She wanted to both get the information out and, ask about it in juxtaposition with his vast experience. Todd said he had an AA degree in criminal justice. Most experts in his field had a PhD in fire sciences or chemistry. Once Jordon revealed that vulnerability, she was able to get to his experience. Todd had been called in to investigate over 3,000 fires. He testified he'd determined that less than one tenth of those were arsons, and after investigating those, he concluded less than half of the suspected arsons produced enough evidence to pursue criminal charges. Over the course of 16 years, Todd had arrested approximately 80 alleged arsonists.

Once Jordon felt she'd hit hard on Todd's prudent tendencies, as well as his wealth of experience, she decided to ask the million dollar questions. She wanted to make her major points while the jury was still fresh. After that, she'd backfill with the more technical inquires.

"Inspector Petersen, did you investigate a fire that occurred on August 17, 2004?"

"Yes, I," Todd was quick to correct her, "along with the other team members."

Jordon had intentionally asked the question that way, knowing Todd would quickly correct her and give credit to his staff. Jordon wanted his magnanimous nature to come through; she knew it would further endear him to the jury.

"And as a result of this investigation," Jordon asked, "did you, and *your team*, talk about possible causes of the fire?"

"Yes, actually we engaged in some rather lively discussions about that."

Once again, Jordon counted on Todd correcting her. She knew he didn't want the jury to think they just casually came to their conclusions.

"And did you form an opinion as to what the cause of this fire was?"

"Yes, ultimately, but not before we discussed all possible scenarios and continuously challenged each other's hypotheses."

"I see." Jordon's perceptible level of interest made it appear as if she were learning about this process for the first time. In truth, she'd been involved in the legal aspects of this investigation right from the beginning. "Still," Jordon continued, "despite your collective process, doesn't one person have to make the final call?"

"Yes."

"And who would that be?" Jordon knew the jury would already surmise who, and she wanted to give them the experience of being right.

"That would be me," Todd answered, but promptly added, "because I am ultimately responsible for all our conclusions."

Jordon knew he didn't want to appear conceited. He just wanted them to know he was prepared to be held accountable. "And did you make such a determination in this case?" she asked.

"Yes."

"And what did you decide?"

Todd turned to face the jury. "That this lethal fire was intentionally set, it was in fact an arson."

Jordon paused; Todd didn't stop looking into the eyes of the jury until Jordon asked her next question. They both wanted the jury to experience Todd's integrity and sincerity.

Jordon looked over at the jury, she was right, they were hooked. They all looked alert, some were even leaning forward in their chairs. Okay, she thought, time to backfill; if I wait even a second longer our staged moment will appear staged.

"What," she asked, "led you to believe this fire was in fact an arson and not an accident?"

"The evidence," Todd answered. "All of the evidence collected, both from the scene, and from the autopsy, suggests this was a fast moving fire; hence an arson. Had the fire begun with a small, accidental flame," Todd continued, "say from a cigarette, a lit candle, or a spark, it would have burned slowly. Had it burned slowly Miss Gold's CoHb level would have been significantly higher, her fingers would likely have been singed rather than destroyed, there would have been more soot deposits near the orifices of her face, and she would not have died as a result of a laryngospasm.

"On the other hand, the arson investigation team never found a trace of the igniter that was used; we therefore assumed it all burned in the fire. We also never found any specific forensic evidence that proves who the arsonist was. Still, there was a plethora of evidence collected by my team to prove that this was in fact an arson. Shall I go on?"

***

Todd had been waiting for this moment for many months. Although in general he was a soft spoken, quiet man, Todd loved talking about his team's arson investigations, and as far as he was concerned it didn't get any better than 12 people who could technically be arrested if they left during his discourse.

***

Todd and Jordon then began their programmed questions and answers. They used simple photographs, charts, and actual objects found at the scene. Everything was shown to the jury in as comprehensive and illustrative manner as possible.

One such display began with a photo of the bedroom, followed by a close-up of the bed, and then a close-up of the corner of the bed. This series of photographs focused on a frayed and burnt fragment of the bedspread. The next photo was of a forensic investigator carefully removing this fragment from the bed. This was followed by a series of photos showing how the investigator took this material, carefully mounted it on a piece of white cardboard and then sealed it with clear plastic wrap.

Finally, the real fragment was introduced, at which point Jordon stopped her questioning as the packaged evidence was passed from one juror to another.

Todd and Jordon had spent days perfecting their presentation. As Jordon watched the jury pass the fragment around, she felt they had reached their goal; as much as possible, they made the jurors feel as if they were actually at the crime scene, interpreting the evidence the same way Todd did.

Once Todd finished explaining what he'd learned from his investigation of Miss Gold's home, Jordon introduced photos taken from inside West's tool shed.

The shed was filled with lanterns, gas cans, stoves, and other incendiary devises. After the jury saw these photos, each object was then hand-carried by a uniformed Fire-fighter into the courtroom. The sheer number and smell was overwhelming - just as they had hoped.

As Todd's direct examination progressed, Jordon felt each segment flowed naturally from the one before. Eventually, the examination culminated in a Power Point presentation. During the presentation, Todd was able, using his laser pen, to highlight "burn pattern indicators" in order to illustrate to the jury where the furniture originally stood, how quickly the fire moved, and what objects succumbed first. Jordon thought even Judge Ames appeared impressed.

When Jordon finally said, "No further questions," she was convinced the jury was all theirs.

The first part of Phillip Adler's cross-examination was predictable and unimaginative. Jordon listened cautiously for the first few minutes, but once it became apparent that every time Todd opened his mouth he helped the prosecution, Jordon just sat back and enjoyed watching one of her favorite colleagues harass a worthy opponent.

Shortly thereafter, according to Volume I of the transcript, they broke for the "noon recess."

***

Saturday, April 4, 2006 2 p.m.

When Jordon put down Volume I of the transcript, she decided she also needed a break.

As she stood up, some muscles in her leg began to cramp. She hobbled around until the cramping diminished. Going from the run directly back to her desk, she decided, was not a good idea. Time for a shower, or better yet - a hot tub!

Jordon took off her running clothes, put on a robe, and went outside to uncover the tub. Taking off the heavy hard top, by herself, was both difficult and awkward. Jordon wondered how Greg always managed to do it without complaining. By the time she finally leaned it up against the side of the wall, Jordon appreciated Greg all the more, which made her feel all the more guilty.

As soon as Jordon turned around, she cringed and backed up, the area was now permeated with hot, chlorine-drenched air.

Seconds later, the air cleared and the tub looked perfect. Jordon un-zipped her robe, climbed in, sank down, leaned back, closed her eyes, and burst out laughing. She was remembering the lunch she shared with Todd and Jake the day Todd testified.

***

Monday, November 4, 2006 12:15 p.m.

That noon, Jordon, Jake and Todd decided to celebrate Todd's successful morning by dining at their favorite restaurant, Bonjour. Bonjour was a French bistro located not far from the courthouse, but its ambiance always made them feel as if they'd been transported a continent away.

As they walked up Bonjour's gleaming white steps, the outdoor speakers greeted them with the melodious voice of Maurice Chevalier. "Thank Heaven for Little Girls," Maurice sang; inspiring Jake, in concurrence with the crooner's words, to ask Jordon to dance.

Jordon giggled and turned him down. Jake then looked at Todd, who bowed and acquiesced. Suddenly Jake and Todd were tangoing up the remaining steps. Jordon looked around; and, seeing no jurors, she let her giggle quickly grow into a full guffaw.

Once inside, they were welcomed by the effusive, energetic Albert DeBelle, the restaurant's owner. Albert ushered them to what they considered to be "their area," in the back. "Their area" had a screen blocking it off from the rest of the restaurant and a couch on each side of the low table. En route, Jordon veered off to the bathroom. When she returned, she sat next to Todd. Both men looked surprised. Jordon didn't think she'd been *that* obvious in seizing every chance she had to sit next to Jake, yet, her investigators kept staring at her in search of an explanation.

"I, I need to show Todd some of my re-direct questions."

"Oh bullshit," Todd offered, "you just like me better."

"Does not!" Jake replied in his most macho-juvenile voice.

"Does so!" Was Todd's not so creative reply.

As if spring-loaded, both men instantly shot up, puffed out their chests and put up their fists. Meanwhile, Jordon laughed. Then, after a few more predictable retorts, Jordon stood up and joined the fray. Suddenly, they were all talking at once. Most of their sentences began with, "Well you…" and ended with a description of some silly idiosyncrasy each thought the other had. Throughout the fracas, their laughter and voices elevated. Suddenly Albert arrived and appeared shocked. They froze. Once Albert left they dropped down on to the couches and their cackling continued. Every once in a while one of the three would sober up, causing the others to do whatever it took to get them going again.

Church laughter was the term Jordon thought of. It was the kind of laughter that was inappropriate, both because of its timing as well as its volume. It was during these moments in life that Jordon knew she shouldn't be laughing but laughing felt so good, in part because it was so bad, that she decided to just go with it.

That afternoon their collective *church laughter* helped dissipate the pressure they'd all been under for a very long time. At some point, Jordon looked up and appreciated the screen all the more. Eventually the waitress arrived and they ordered. The guys requested matching Monte Carlo sandwiches and she ordered a *salade nicose*. Mid-way through their meal, Jake reached under the table and briefly squeezed Jordon's knee; Jordon felt instantly turned on. The effect of the imprint of his strong hand lingered long after he pulled it away.

***

Now, lying in the hot-tub, Jordon felt turned on just thinking about it. She quickly stood up. "Back to work, Danner!" She got out, toweled off, and retuned to the transcript of Todd's surprisingly painful afternoon session.

***

Monday, November 4, 2005 1:33 p.m.

Todd was back on the stand. Within moments, Jordon realized while they spent their lunch hour eating French food and rolling around on a couch, the defense attorney had spent his time preparing for the afternoon session and revamping his strategy. Adler, Jordon concluded, came back with a vengeance. Having figured out he couldn't attack the investigation, he clearly decided to attack the investigator. But, she thought, he's going to have to be careful; if the jury feels Todd is being unjustifiably assaulted, they'll turn on Adler.

The afternoon session dragged on. After spending a reasonable amount of time pointing out Todd's lack of formal education, Adler then asked about every debatable call Todd had ever made in his career. Obviously, Adler had done his homework, and, as much as she wanted to, Jordon knew she couldn't object to this barrage of questions. Adler's questions, she concluded, were technically within the boundaries of the very low legal standard of "good faith." And although she felt none of Todd's answers gave the defense much, she knew the sheer number was bound to give the jury pause.

In the end, Jordon thought, what really hurt them was not Adler's questions, but Todd's reactions. Todd got defensive and lost his cool.

By the time Jordon was asked if she had any re-direct questions it was late in the day and the jury looked exhausted. Jordon carefully weighed the jury's apparent fatigue, with the mileage she could get out of Todd's answers on re-direct. She also considered Todd's feelings.

Jordon knew he would want her to re-ask about everything so he could explain away all the discrepancies and inconsistencies, but Jordon knew she had to read the jury and then do what she thought was best for their case. Jordon chose to briefly "rehabilitate" Todd and then stop.

"You previously indicated," Jordon began, "you have investigated three thousand fires, correct?"

"Yes," he answered, "at least that many."

"During the course of those investigations, approximately how many judgment calls did you have to make per fire?"

"I couldn't be more precise than to estimate - dozens?"

"Okay, so maybe twenty-four per fire?"

"At least."

"So, at least twenty-four per fire and you've investigated at least three thousand fires. So, that's at least seven thousand two hundred judgment calls over the course of your career as an investigator, correct?"

"At the very least."

Jordon looked over at the jury, most seemed as if they were back on board; she was glad she had chosen a perceptive lot. Jordon hoped to win the rest over with the next few questions.

"By my count, Mr. Adler asked you about fourteen of those judgment calls, some of them going back approximately a dozen or so years ago. Does that sound about right to you?"

"Actually I think his questions concerned thirteen different judgment calls going back nearly fifteen years."

Good, she thought, Todd's getting some of his confidence back.

"Fair enough," she responded. "Of those thirteen calls did you feel each time, at the moment you made your decision, that your decision was correct?"

"Yes, at the time, given the information I had at that moment, I did, and still do, feel the decisions I made were appropriate."

"Well, were you right each time?"

"No, I was right about half the time in those thirteen incidences."

"Who decided you were ultimately wrong?"

"Me."

"What made you decide that?"

"Later, once I obtained more information, I amended some of my thinking so as to include the new evidence, but still, even in those situations, my ultimate opinion as to the cause and path those fires took, remained unchanged."

"Has your ultimate opinion in this case ever changed?"

"No, not once, not even after I studied all the data and poked holes in all the hypotheses, including my own."

"And in this case did you personally review most of the data?"

"In *this* case, I personally reviewed *all* of the data."

"Do you always do that?"

"No."

"Then why did you do that this time?"

"Because, Ms. Danner, someone died."

Jordon stayed silent for an extra moment; she wanted to let his last response sink in, and his next one stand out.

"Inspector Peterson, has *anything* Mr. Adler asked you, made you doubt, *in any way*, your conclusion that this fire was an arson?"

"No."

"Thank you. Your Honor, I have nothing further."

Adler wasn't about to let her have the last word. He rose and asked, "Mr. Peterson, you're not trying to manipulate this jury into believing you're perfect are you?"

"No, Mr. Adler, I'm telling the truth; manipulation seems to be your mission."

Although Todd's words sounded strong he looked wounded.

"I have no further questions of *this witness*," was Adler's only response.

Adler, Jordon thought, must have liked Todd's expression and feared he'd fully rehabilitate himself if another question was asked. Meanwhile, Jordon liked Todd's last words, and wanted to leave them lingering in the jury's mind; so, she too asked no further questions.

Todd was dismissed.

As Todd left the stand he avoided looking into the jurors' eyes. Walking past Jordon he gave her a glance of discontentment.

Once the inner courtroom door shut, Judge Ames excused the jury for the day.

Packing up their files Jordon leaned over to Jake and asked, "Am I being paranoid or–"

"Nope," Jake answered rushing out, "I'm going to try to catch up to him and get him to meet us for a drink. I'll see you there."

There was no need to say where "there" was.

***

They were to meet in the only local bar where the deck extended over the ocean. Jordon arrived first.

Because of the day's low clouds, an explosive sunset was brewing. From the moment Todd and Jake arrived Jordon noticed Todd avoided all eye contact with her. Still, she decided to wait until their beers came before confronting him.

Once he had his beer in hand, Jordon asked, "Okay Toddy," it was a name she often affectionately used for him, "what's up?"

It was apparently all the opening he needed. "Why," he asked, "didn't you go through each of those thirteen judgment calls? I could've–"

Jordon interrupted him. After a hard afternoon in court and having already consumed most of her beer, she was feeling righteously defensive. "Because," she said, "it would've bored the hell out of the jury."

"Bullshit! I think the jury would have been interested in knowing why I decided what I did, when I did."

"No Todd, I think that was what *you* were interested in. And you know as well as I do, because you have reminded me of it many times, this case isn't about you or me or Jake, it's about Ruthie. And it's about making sure justice is served, not our egos."

"Jordon, this isn't just about my ego, it's about my future. From now on I can count on being impeached with each of those thirteen calls *every* time I testify."

"Maybe so, but I can't run my trial worrying about my friends or what may or may not happen to them the next time they testify," Jordon reached over the table and grabbed his hand, "as much as I may want to." Jordon finally got him to look at her. "Anyway, Todd; it wasn't his questions that hurt us, it was the way you answered them. You got defensive." Todd withdrew his hand and was about to respond, but she cut him off. "Todd, the jury was looking to you to see if it was a big deal, and just by your gestures and tone you told them it was. I couldn't risk you coming across on redirect as self-protective, or me appearing as if I'd lost my objectivity."

Jordon kept her eyes on Todd while he looked past her towards the afterglow of the setting sun. Jordon felt terrible letting down her friend and afterward could only hope she'd made the right decision. Although she knew she was about to sound more confident than she felt, she added, "Todd, I think what I accomplished on redirect was to show the jury again what a professional you are. By the time they left today, there was no doubt in any of their minds that this fire was investigated thoroughly by a top-notch investigative team, headed by Senior Inspector Todd Peterson."

Todd didn't respond. Jordon thought he was considering what she'd just said. Jordon reached across the table, took both of his hands, and looked into his eyes; she wanted to make her adoration of him obvious.

A moment later, Todd gave her an almost imperceptible smile. "You forgot to add incredibly handsome to your description of this Senior Inspector."

Jordon knew she was forgiven.

A visibly relieved Jake slapped both of his hands on the table and rejoiced, "Time for a group hug!"

"Screw the group hug," Todd's real smile returned. "I'm milking this for all its worth and hugging Jordon all on my own."

Todd's comment, once again, resulted in a silly-macho exchange between Todd and Jake, which Jordon ended by pushing Jake away and giving Todd a warm, long-lasting embrace. Jake, of course, ceremoniously pouted, and then all three of them laughed. Soon Jordon called over their waitress and insisted on paying for the next round. Todd agreed she should, calling her 'Brutus' and claiming that it was the least she could do. In response Jordon lifted her legal pad and said, "Hail Caesar," as she swatted Todd over the head.

***

Now, surrounded by the comfort of her log home, Jordon reconsidered that conversation with Todd and concluded she'd crossed the line and was in fact, "brutally honest." Brutally honest was a phrase one of her college acquaintances used to describe Jordon's callousness. Jordon never meant to be callous, but she knew at times she was. She knew her directness should, on occasion, be tempered, but sometimes, she just lost control. She loved working with Todd and hoped, upon reflection, he'd think she'd done the right thing. For her part, she was still fretful. She hated when her passion, in this situation for seeking justice, blurred her concern for those she loved.

Jordon knew Todd was on a long weekend mountain biking trip when the hung jury came back. She thought they should call him on his cell phone, but Jake wanted to wait. They finally agreed that even though Todd would initially feel left out if they didn't get in touch, in the end he'd be glad he got to enjoy the rest of his trip. Meanwhile, Jordon was sure if they went to trial again they could handle Todd's "judgment calls" on direct examination, and even if the defense attorney went for the jugular on that, or any other issue, Todd could handle it and would never lose his cool again.

Todd was the quintessential professional; Jordon just wished all the experts, in all of her cases, could be as much as half as good as him, which brought her back to the Cantera case.

After her last experience with Dr. Rhinehart, Jordon decided to be especially careful in reviewing Dr. Davidson's reports.

Sandy Davidson was the doctor who had performed Diana's sexual assault examination. Jordon had always liked Sandy, because she cared deeply about *her* sexual assault victims and wanted to bring them both health and justice. Fortunately for Jordon, Sandy also believed each of those concepts were intertwined. Regrettably, some other doctors Jordon had contact with, in other cases, felt their exclusive job was to address their patients' medical needs, which did not include testifying in court on their behalf. Sandy, on the other hand, had a more classic view of medicine. She thought testifying aided her patients healing process and served as preventative medicine for the entire community.

20

Saturday, October 20, 2005 4:45 a.m.

Medicine – The science and art dealing with the prevention, cure, and alleviation of diseases; in a narrower sense that part of the science and art of restoring and preserving health.

Shortly before 5 o'clock Diana was discharged from the emergency room and wheeled across the street to the Sexual Assault Response Team building. Once at S.A.R.T., the forensic nurse decided Diana was still legally incapable of "knowingly" signing the consent form; therefore, the medical/legal exam had to be delayed.

Twenty minutes after Diana arrived at S.A.R.T., Lourdes, a rape crisis volunteer, joined them. Throughout the remainder of the ordeal, Lourdes never left Diana's side.

When Diana could finally sit up, she kept shaking and insisted upon staying tightly wrapped in the hospital blanket. Although at times she appeared oriented and weepy, she still couldn't give them sequential information, or the phone numbers of anyone she wanted called.

By the time Dr. Sandy Davidson walked in, Diana was sitting on the edge of the examination table. At first glance, Sandy thought Diana had been badly beaten. Upon closer examination, she noted that the grotesque discoloration around Diana's eyes was just smeared make-up.

Sandy wiped off Diana's make-up, and waited. Everyone present understood the genital exam would not begin until Dr. Davidson could understand her patient's slurred speech.

The exam was finally performed at 5:54 a.m. Although Diana's signature was still indecipherable, those present felt she understood what she was signing. The first forensic observation Sandy made was noting the fingernail scratch marks on the sides of Diana's body. In response, Sandy briefly stepped out of the room and told the waiting deputy to call his colleagues to remind them to scrape under the suspect's nails.

When Sandy returned to the examination room, Lourdes told her that Diana really wanted Sandy to know how sorry Diana was.

"Diana," Sandy said in a soft and conciliatory voice, "this *wasn't* your fault and we're just glad you're here and safe. For now, rest. We'll talk more about what happened in a little while."

During the remaining part of her medical exam, Dr. Davidson collected biological evidence and photographed Diana's injuries, both large and small.

The medical report included diagrams showing Diana had abrasions on her back that were longer than 4 inches and genital lacerations that were no larger than 2 centimeters. The report also indicated that Diana's hymen appeared to have been torn. Subsequent lab reports revealed that the only intoxicating agent present in her system was alcohol, which was found at, "extremely high levels."

Once Diana was dressed, Sandy got Diana's permission to videotape the interview.

***

Jordon began the tape. Dr. Davidson, Lourdes, and Diana were all sitting together in an autumn-colored chamber located right next door to the examination room.

This would be the third time Jordon was to review the tape. By now she'd talked to both Sandy and Diana about what they said and why.

***

"Can you tell me what happened?" Sandy asked.
Diana didn't respond.

"Can you tell me what sex acts were attempted or accomplished by your assailant?" Sandy asked the question as it was stated on her mandated form; she was obviously trying to so it in as soft and non-judgmental a tone as possible.

"My assailant?" Diana asked.

"Yes, your assailant - the person who sexually assaulted you." Sandy was merely defining assailant.

"The person who sexually assaulted me?" Diana asked.

"Yes, what did he do?"

"He assaulted me." Diana had no idea what she was saying, but she didn't want to appear the drunken fool she was.

"How did he sexually assault you?" Sandy continued asking the questions, having no way of knowing her patient was too proud to say 'I don't know.'

"He sexually assaulted me." Diana repeated.

"Did he use his hands?"

"Yes." Diana's eyes began to slowly dart around.

"How?"

"I'm not sure."

"You're not sure or you don't want to say?" Sandy appeared calm and understanding.

"I don't want to say." Diana was happy to have an excuse not to make things up.

"Did he put his finger inside of you?"

She dropped her head down, "inside of me," she repeated.

"Did he use his penis?"

"Yes."

"How?"

"Same way."

"Inside of you?"

"Inside of me."

"How about his mouth?"

"His mouth?"

"Yes, his mouth."

Diana looked up. "Do you mean did he kiss me?"

"Well, yes. Okay, did he kiss you - anywhere?"

Diana looked indignant. "I wouldn't let him kiss me."

"Oh, okay," Dr. Davidson said, "we're going to turn off the tape now."

***

Saturday April 5, 2006 4:05 P.M.

And that, Jordon thought once again, is their best evidence. The defense will use that tape to prove Diana knew she'd been assaulted, and therefore was not too intoxicated to give consent. Additionally, they will argue that since she said she wouldn't let him kiss her, and, according to her statement to Sandy, he didn't, it proves she had, and used, the power to stop him.

In reality, Diana remembered nothing about the assault and lied during her interview with Sandy Davidson; she did it just to save face. But how, Jordon worried, am I ever going to convince the jury to trust a liar? The jury will have to understand Diana felt too humiliated to tell the truth. But why would Diana feel she had to lie about being too drunk to remember? The only answer Jordon had come up with was that Diana didn't want anyone to know about her drinking habits, because, Jordon speculated, at the time of her rape, Diana was a closet alcoholic, who was perhaps experiencing a black-out.

Although Diana never told anyone how often she drank, her blood alcohol level that night was exorbitantly high. As far as Jordon knew, only "experienced drinkers" could have a B.A. level that high and still function. Additionally, Jordon had learned that having a perfect appearance was not only a major part of who Diana was, it was also what her future career dictated.

Jordon needed answers, so she had brought along a few articles recommended by The California Council on Alcoholism. Now, she decided, was the time to read them.

Jordon stood up and walked over to the box containing the articles but when she knelt down, she decided she couldn't quite bring herself to search for them. I guess, she concluded, I need a break from thinking about Diana. I suppose I just don't want to find out what I already know.

As she stood back up, she decided instead to call the Santa Barbara County Jail.

21

Saturday April 4, 2006 10:00 a.m.

Pornographic – That which is obscene.

After Muratoto hung up, Arty went into the living room and turned on his computer. A moment later he opened a file he'd named "College Cuties." Arty clicked on the name - "D." Up sprang an image of Diana having sex with Arty's friend, Ernesto Cantera.

Arty stepped away from the computer and began to pace; he had to come up with a plan. The case against Cantera couldn't go to trial, not now, not with Muratoto suddenly sounding suspicious.

Arty pressed "PRINT"; he decided to personally take the photos to Diana. He'd tell her if she cooperated with the cops, he'd put these photos on the internet. If that didn't stop her, he'd have come up with something else.

Arty dressed quickly and then returned to his computer to look up the address of her TV station. Before leaving he grabbed all but the last of the still-printing photos.

22

Saturday April 5, 2006 4:15 p.m.

California Evidence Code Section 1024 – Exception to patient and psychotherapist privilege – There is no privilege under this article if the psychotherapist has reasonable cause to believe that the patient is in such mental condition as to be dangerous to another, and that disclosure of the communication is necessary to prevent the threatened danger.

"Jail administration, Sergeant Bass speaking."

"Ron, what are you doing working at the jail?" Ron and Jordon were long-time acquaintances. His regular job was working as a bailiff in what Jordon considered to be the least friendly criminal courtroom in Santa Barbara County.

"I decided to pick up some O.T.," Ron answered. "It's easy money; I mostly just monitor the visitations. So, what do you need?"

Jordon could tell Ron already felt imposed upon just having to answer the phone. "Can you get me some info on whether one of my defendant's has placed any new calls since Friday?"

"Can't that wait until the regular guy is in, on Monday?" Ron asked.

"No," was Jordon's complete reply.

"Okay, so who's the inmate?"

"Alexandra West."

"Ahh, Dragon lady - hang on."

The Correction Officers usually had pet names for their high profile defendants. Jordon could only assume this one had something to do with Alexandra being an arsonist.

A few minutes later Ron returned to the phone. "Nope, not a one."

"Okay, well, thanks for checking." Jordon couldn't keep the disappointment out of her voice.

"Hey, hang on a minute. Don't you think you should have asked me if she had a visitor?"

Jordon was certain her heart stopped. "Who?"

"Hang on."

Jordon could barely contain herself. If this visitor was anyone but her lawyer, this could be another great lead.

Ron returned to the phone. "It was a shrink, a Doctor Swimmer. She came in early this morning. The good doctor looked distinguished, but seemed pretty riled up. Matter of fact, twice she told me she was a doctor - a psychiatrist and that they had doctor-patient privilege, so I shouldn't listen to or record their talk. Well, I'll tell you, I had to try pretty darn hard *not* to listen, this was one pissed off shrink and she was very busy giving her supposed patient the what for. Well anyway, I didn't hear anything, but I did ask her for proof that she was a Doc and she gave me her card." Ron paused for a moment. "Here it is; it's got her address and phone number on it. So, do you want those things?"

"Hell yes!" Jordon replied. Even the crankiest of law enforcement officers, Jordon decided, still had their shinning moments.

Ron read the card, in its entirety, and Jordon thanked him multiple times.

As soon as Jordon hung up she pressed "FLASH" and began to dial Swimmer's number.

"This is Dr. Doris Swimmer. I will be out of the office today; however, I will be checking my messages. You are invited to leave a message after the tone."

Wanting a return call that day, Jordon was determined to leave a vague yet urgent sounding communiqué.

"Doctor Swimmer. This is Jordon Danner, the D.A. of Santa Barbara County." Jordon loved using her title at moments like this. "I heard there was some sort of disturbance at the jail this morning and you were a part of it. You can call and talk to me about it on Monday, or *you are invited* to call me anytime today." Jordon left the number and was confident the good doctor would be calling back soon. She was sure no doctor wanted a weekend call from the District Attorney asserting that their name had been associated with a disturbance at the jail.

As soon as Jordon hung up she began rubbing her face and forehead. What, she wondered, went down during West and Swimmer's excited conversation? What would make a distinguished looking shrink go ballistic at someone in jail? Jordon unconsciously glanced up at the clock. "Damn I'm starving, twelve minutes to five - almost five hours past lunchtime!"

What she really wanted was thick salami on rye with plenty of deli mustard. What she prepared was a can of healthy vegetable soup; she felt she had to. She might be going back into trial in a month.

To successfully prosecute a case, Jordon felt she had to first learn everything about it - all of the facts, as well as the law, and if anywhere along the way she formed a reasonable doubt, she had to dismiss the charges. However, if she went forward, it would mean she was both personally and professionally convinced of the defendant's culpability. Once she made that decision, she felt she needed to package both herself and her evidence in a way that invited the jury to closely scrutinize each. For Jordon that meant she had to feel healthy, exude confidence, and look good. She knew most people thought she was at times obsessed with these goals, but she preferred to think of herself as steadfast and focused. She hoped she was right about that, because at the moment she didn't feel particularly healthy, steadfast or focused; she felt out of control.

True to her nature, Jordon started drinking the soup before it had sufficiently cooled down. Throughout her life Jordon had never been a patient person and was often 'burnt' by her eagerness. This time she was saved by the ringing phone. Ahh, she thought, the good doctor.

"Hello"

"Ordon Danna?"

It was an unknown male's voice.

"Yes; who's this?"

There was no response, but she could hear someone breathing. "This is Jordon Danner," she repeated. The caller hung up.

Jordon always hated hang-ups like that, but with no ability to *69 someone from the antiquated mountain phone system, she was stuck with not knowing who the caller, with the strange accent, was.

A moment later the phone rang again. Jordon answered poised for battle.

"This is Jordon Danner."

"Yes, Ms. Danner, this is Doctor Swimmer. I just got your message." Dr. Swimmer now adopted Jordon's snappish tone. "Why are you calling me about what should have been a private conversation between my patient and me?"

"Doctor, I don't know what you and the *inmate* said to each other, nor do I know if she is your patient. The information conveyed to me was that there was a disturbance at the jail this morning between you and an inmate. As you may or may not know, I am prosecuting that individual, and as far as I knew, she didn't have a psychiatrist. Certainly there are no jail records of you having called or visited before. Now, perhaps you were just hired, or she is your patient and there's been no record of it. If either is true, then she is your patient, but if you haven't been retained, then there is no doctor-patient privilege–"

"*I* asserted the privilege, on behalf of my client, while I was there," Swimmer interrupted her, "therefore your goons should not have listened to or taped our visit–"

"As far as I know," this time Jordon interrupted her, "no one did either. As to whether you lawfully asserted that privilege," Jordon slowed her speech down, "I'll put that issue aside, *for now*." Jordon knew she was coming very close to the line. In essence, what she was doing was threatening Swimmer with criminal prosecution, or at the very least, an investigation. She knew she was now on a questionable "fishing expedition," and because she felt that the only lawful means she had to get access to what Dr. Swimmer knew was to remind her of 1024, Jordon decided to mention it and just see what happened next. *"For now,"* Jordon continued, "I'm only going to ask you if you are familiar with your obligation under Evidence Code Section ten-twenty-four."

"Of course I am!" Swimmer erupted using a voice punched with righteous indignation, "And, I am also aware that under ten-twenty-four, I can only give the warning directly to the alleged victim, which is something I already did - in writing!"

Suddenly there was silence.

Jordon quickly considered how she should proceed; her conclusion was, with great caution. She did not want to be sued, or worse, disbarred. "Doctor Swimmer," Jordon began hesitantly, "you warned Ruth Gold that Alexandra was going to kill her?"

"You know," Dr. Swimmer whispered, "I can't tell *you* that."

"Doctor Swimmer, if such a warning was sent to Ruthie's home, even a day before her death, law enforcement had a warrant that allowed them access to that letter." Jordon held her breath; she knew she was on shaky ground because it was beginning to sound as if Alexandra was Swimmer's patient even before the arrest.

"Doctor Swimmer," Jordon's voice was beginning to change from hesitant to begging. *"If* you sent such a document to Ms. Gold, for God's sake, please fax a copy to me."

There was no reply.

Jordon knew Dr. Swimmer probably shouldn't say or do anything else. Swimmer too could be sued, or worse, lose her license. Still if Swimmer followed the news, as Jordon suspected she did, it had probably inspired her unprecedented visit to the jail, and it just might mean that Swimmer too hated the idea of Alexandra West getting away with murder.

"What's your fax number?"

Nine minutes later, Dr. Swimmer's letter to Ruthie began to sputter out of Jordon's printer. Jordon stood by like a nervous expectant father. The letter was brief and to the point. The missive was dated two days before Ruthie's murder. It said that Dr. Swimmer was Alexandra West's treating psychiatrist and that Ms. West had made some threatening statements about elderly people in general and Ruthie in particular. The letter ended by saying Ruthie should take whatever precautions she deemed necessary.

Jordon held the flimsy fax in her hands as she pictured Ruthie's charred body. Ruthie never had a chance, Jordon thought; Ruthie never received this letter, because if she had, Jordon's eyes filled with tears, Ruthie would never have gone to brunch with Alexandra that morning.

Jordon went into the bathroom to splash cold water on her face.

No doubt about it, Jordon thought as she dried her hands, Dragon Lady confiscated the letter and now I've got to find the original. It's not likely I can use this fax given the way I got it, and even if I find the original, it might just be deemed inadmissible hearsay.

Jordon's next call was to the Watch Commander's office.

"Watch Commander's office Hadley speaking."

"Hey Kirk, Jordon Danner here."

"Hey Jordon, bummer about that hung jury of yours. Something I can do for you?"

"Yes, and thanks, I need one of the evidence guys to come in, open the evidence room, and look through some of the paper work in my case. I need to find a letter, and I'd like it this weekend."

"Let me see what I can do. Raul and Saul are the only ones allowed to go in there. I'll see if I can reach either one. Technically they're only suppose to come in on weekends if they're needed to *process* evidence, not to look for it...but, like I said, let me see what I can do. Meanwhile tell me what you're looking for, I'll relay the message to them, and get back to you either way."

Jordon gave him the case number and the evidence tag integer for the bag marked "misc. paperwork/suspect's apartment." Jordon also gave him the date of the letter and who it was from.

After Jordon hung up she carefully considered the new evidence. She'd have to get the original letter; the circumstances surrounding her getting the fax were too murky. Once they found the original letter. Her legal theory of admissibility would be that the defendant's statements to Dr. Swimmer were evidence of the defendant's "Pre-existing State of Mind;" Jordon just hope the judge would buy that argument.

Regardless, Jordon couldn't wait to tell Jake about the new twist in their case, but she also knew at this moment he was out of range. All she could do now was leave him a message to call her right away, but she knew he'd do that anyway.

After leaving him the message she began pacing again. Now, what the hell was I doing before that flurry of activity? Oh yeah, right - I was going to take a look at that alcohol blackout material. I guess I was having a blackout. Jordon started to laugh out loud at her own weak joke. Between her lack of sleep and many pulls in multiple directions she was starting to get punchy.

A moment later, Jake called to announce he had just about finished his work in Wichita and would catch the 'red eye' back. Jordon told him about the letter: at first, he was thrilled and then, angry. "Whose assignment," he asked, "was it to read through all the miscellaneous paperwork?"

"I don't remember, but I'm guessing one of the detectives breezed through it and asked one of the cadets to actually read everything. That's the way it's usually done."

"Well, then it's my fault if we missed that letter the first time around. This is my investigation and everything should have been gone over carefully. Did we give the defense an opportunity to see everything we took from West's home?"

"Yep." That was one of Jordon's first concerns; she didn't want to be accused of withholding evidence. "Remember? A month after we collected all the evidence we had the defense attorney and his investigator come to the Police Department. Once there Matt U. and Matt S. laid all the bags of evidence on tables and gave them hours to look through it. Of course, one of our guys was in the room at all times."

"Okay," Jake sighed, "so if it's there, we can use it, right?"

"Probably," she answered.

"Ahh, come on, you'll figure out a way to get it in - you always do. I just feel like an idiot for missing it the first time."

Jordon decided now was not the time to explain the legal minutiae of hearsay evidence in juxtaposition with the doctor/patient privilege rule. If they found the original letter, she'd take it from there. For now, she just didn't want Jake to berate himself further.

"Jake, let it go. We both know you're the best." Jordon smiled but could sense he didn't. Jordon knew Jake was very hard on himself, he expected nothing less than perfection, which was why she also knew his falling in love with a married woman, was killing him. Jordon wanted to put him out of his misery; she cared about him too much to see him suffer. "Jake, we do need to talk about us."

"I know, but not now. I'm pissed, I'm beat, and I need to concentrate on tracking down Ming. Maybe I can redeem myself by finding the last piece of evidence; the piece that truly nails West's coffin shut. Regardless, I've got to try. I'll stay in touch and meanwhile, congrats on your latest discovery, Sherlock, that could just do it. Take care Babe."

The telephone line went dead.

Babe, Jordon thought, again with the Babe, and again my whole body responds. Okay, now I definitely need a distraction: where the hell is that Blackout article anyway?

***

Jake flicked his cell phone shut and jammed it into its case. He heard the clip crack, but was too angry to look at it. How the hell, he wondered, did I miss that letter? And if I missed that, what the hell else did I miss?

Jake stood up and started pacing. I need to get back to Santa Barbara, interview Ming, and then spend the night in the damn evidence room. I need to look at each piece of paper and every shred of evidence. This is totally unacceptable! I really fucked this up...I always thought my feelings toward Jordon made me work this case harder; now I think it might have distracted me. This is bullshit. This should never have happened!

Jake grew up believing he had to be twice as good as everyone else because he was half their color. He couldn't just be an athlete; he had to be a scholar-athlete. For Jake it wasn't enough to be the senior class president; he had to be the senior class president who spent Christmas Eve serving up dinner at a homeless shelter. Jake always felt he had to be perfect; it seemed to please everyone who surrounded him, that is everyone but his mother Clarisse.

Jake now thought back to all the nights when he'd been up late doing his homework, and she'd been up late working on a project. Sometimes she'd come into his room and they'd have one of their chats. Clarisse wanted Jake to "go easier" on himself. "We all make mistakes," she'd remind him. He assured her he knew that, but he told himself, not me, I won't let myself make a mistake - and he rarely did.

Early on in Jake's career, he was part of a SWAT raid that confiscated hundreds of assault weapons. It was Jake's job to book the weapons into evidence. As part of the booking process, he had to make sure none of the guns had any bullets remaining inside their chambers. There were 236 weapons in all. The following year, all of the weapons were brought to court for the jury to consider during the trial. The morning they were going to be introduced into evidence a bailiff re-checked the weapons' chambers and found one stray bullet. The bailiff then called Jake and told him, but no one else. Jake immediately reported himself to his sergeant. His sergeant's response was, "I'm glad you came to me, it says a lot about a man's character when he self-reports his mistakes. Now let me tell you something about myself - I try never to make the same mistake three times and I'm going to assume the same about you." Jake appreciated his superior's kind words, but he was confident he'd never make the same mistake even twice.

Now, as far as Jake was concerned, he had. Tomorrow, I'm not leaving that evidence locker without the letter.

***

Jordon went downstairs, found the Blackout file, and brought it upstairs. After making herself a full glass of lemonade with shaved ice and mint, she grabbed the file and went out to the front porch. With both hands full, she had to let the screen door close behind her.

The sound of the slamming door was louder than she expected. Startled, she turned and caught a glimpse of the cranberry colored sunset. Jordon was now both distracted and in awe. She stepped on to the edge of the porch and leaned out until she spotted the anticipated crimson glow on the bark of the birch tree. Jordon loved that image. Unfortunately, next to the birch was the oak tree. The oak, she thought, is in desperate need of a trim. I wonder if Greg has called someone to come to deal with it; he's so great about taking care of things like that, and I'm so neglectful. I don't deserve him.

Jordon sat down on the chaise lounge and leaned back. She then decided to close her eyes just long enough to feel the sun on her face.

Soon thereafter she fell asleep. At some point she dreamed about Sam and the boat.

***

When Jordon woke up, she was chilled and disoriented. She looked down; resting on the floor next to her were an unopened file, and a glass of iceless lemonade with a drowning piece of mint.

23

Saturday, April 4, 2006 11 a.m.

Ignorantia presumitur ubi scientia non probatur - Ignorance is presumed where knowledge is not proved

Muratoto knocked at Arty's apartment door. No one answered; Muratoto kept knocking. Eventually Arty's roommate, Stan, opened the door. Muratoto showed Stan his badge.

"Arty around?" Muratoto asked.

"Nah, I think he left a few minutes ago."

"Know where he went?"

Stan shook his head - no.

"Mind if I come in and ask you a few questions?"

Stan stepped aside and let him in.

As Muratoto walked toward the couch, he saw the last of the Diana/Ernesto photos still lying in the printer tray. Muratoto picked up the photo; his hand began to shake. He showed the photo to Stan. "Know them?"

Muratoto could tell Stan had never seen the photo before. "I, I," Stan began, "I don't know her, but I've seen him around. I think he's a friend of Arty's."

Muratoto began to worry. "Where's Arty now?"

"I don't know man, I wish I did."

24

Saturday, April 5, 2006 6:15 p.m.

Reasonable doubt – A doubt based upon reason and arising from evidence.

Jordon looked over at the file and thought; I've been avoiding this long enough. She decided to start with an article in *The Santa Barbara Independent.* It was written by reporter Matt Kettmann. The article was directed toward the town's newly arrived college students. Kettmann wrote that Dr. Donald Sweeney believed, "A blackout occurs when certain neurotransmitters are inhibited by alcohol that has been broken down by the body. In essence, a blacked-out person does not forget what happened; rather he or she never forms a memory to begin with. Long-term memory and previously learned skills continue to function - enabling conversation, tipsy walking, and basic, though generally poor decision - making. (Still, there is no "working memory.") Ideas and events cannot be stored in the memory bank for more than a few moments. The blacked-out drinker is a functioning zombie, usually for just a few lost hours."

Kettmann went on to say, "Furthermore, Sweeny suggests that a blackout is more likely to occur when a person drinks on an empty stomach, is fatigued, or chugs down beer or booze at a rapid pace."

Jordon knew it was a common belief among experts specializing in this area that blackouts are more likely to occur if the consumer of alcohol is an alcoholic.

As she scanned the rest of the article, Jordon came upon the words that should have been obvious to Diana's friends: "a blacked-out person is more dangerous when left alone."

Jordon knew Diana had no memory of her sexual assault, drank on an almost empty stomach, was fatigued from her busy life in San Francisco, as well as tired from her trip, and had "chugged" much of what she drank.

Jordon spent the next several hours reading through all the material she'd gathered on alcoholism and blackouts. Ultimately, she concluded that in order for her to convince the jury Diana had no memory of the event, and therefore was incapable of giving legal consent to having sex with the defendant, Jordon had to persuade the jury that Diana was experiencing a blackout; and to do that, Diana had to admit to being both dishonest and, if it were true, an alcoholic. Given who Diana was, Jordon knew it would be difficult, if not impossible, for Diana to make either admission, either publicly or privately, but Jordon hoped that for the sake of the case, as well as the sake of Diana's own long-term well-being, she could. As far as her credibility went, Jordon felt that if the jury understood Diana and her addiction, they might appreciate why, when she was speaking to Dr. Davidson, she became so easily confused, or even lied.

One way or another, Jordon was sure she had to deal with what Diana had said to Sandy, and Jordon knew she had to do it during her direct examination or the defense attorney would certainly raise the issue during his cross-examination. After all, if the defense attorney proved Diana's statements to Sandy were inconsistent with someone who had no memory or control over the event, then he could effectively argue that Diana was capable of consenting, and therefore, was lying.

This, Jordon assumed, like most other rape allegations, would be a "he - said, she - said case," and if the jury thought Diana wasn't being fully honest, Jordon would never be able to convince all twelve jurors to convict. Beyond that, Jordon worried, even if they got past this particular hurdle and put Diana through all this discomfort, the jury could still find the defendant not guilty because they would have - a *reasonable doubt.*

In the end Jordon concluded she wanted to give it more thought - the stakes were too high.

Meanwhile, she wondered if Kirk had any luck reaching the evidence room guys, and what, if anything, Jake would be able to come up with on Ming. Jordon looked over at the clock; it was 1 a.m. and definitely time to go to bed.

As she got undressed, Jordon continued to methodically consider everything that was going on, but when she started to fall asleep, all she could do was worry: about her family at sea, and her companion in the air.

25

Saturday, April 5, 2006 8:15 p.m.

Wiretapping – A form of electronic eavesdropping where, upon court order, enforcement officials surreptitiously listen to phone calls.

Arty arrived in San Francisco, called Diana's TV station, and found out she was due there the next day. He considered asking for her cell phone number but decided not to; he didn't want to raise anyone's suspicions. Instead, he resolved to find a cheap hotel, preferably one that offered xxx-rated porn.

***

Muratoto spent the day trying to track down Arty but was unsuccessful. He thought about calling Jordon, but felt he needed more to go on before he involved her. At the end of the day he decided all he could do was to stake out Arty's apartment and put an emergency tap on his phone.

By 8:15 that night, he and his partner, Jeff, were parked outside Arty's complex. Throughout the night, they listened to each phone call going in and out of Arty's apartment.

Shortly after midnight, Arty called. He told Stan he'd gone to San Francisco on business and he'd be back tomorrow night. Stan only told Arty to drive carefully and then he hung up.

Jeff traced the call to a small hotel on Castor Street. Muratoto got behind the wheel of the van and drove the six hours to San Francisco.

26

Sunday April 5, 2006 6 a.m.

Married woman – The legal status of a female who has a husband living and not divorced

Jake arrived back in Santa Barbara at 6 a.m., but decided to wait a few more hours before calling Jordon. He knew she'd hardly slept Friday night and hoped she was sleeping in this morning. No doubt about it, he was worried. Lately she looked sleep and food-deprived. He wanted to take her, take her away, Fiji would be nice.

They'd spend the day on the beach, snorkeling in the immaculate water, swimming with the gleaming, colorful marine life. In the evening, they'd dine only in restaurants that overlooked the beach. She'd wear sleeveless dresses - he loved her arms. At night, well, he couldn't go there, not even in his mind. He'd been *there* in his mind too many times and afterwards he always felt frustrated and guilty.

What the hell was he doing? Jake kept asking himself. She didn't belong to him. She was a *married woman* and he had no right to think of her *that* way.

Jake decided to return to his hotel room, change and go for a run on the beach. He had to clear his head, and then find Ming.

Jake put on a new tight white tee shirt and faded running shorts. As he left he caught a glimpse of himself in the mirror. He knew he looked good. Maybe, he thought, I'll meet the woman of my dreams on my run, but the rub is, I think I already have.

Jake had never known a woman like Jordon; and feared he never would again.

Jake grew up in Boulder. His mother was a much admired professor in the Biology Department at University of Colorado. His father was an emergency room nurse. They had a very happy marriage. Jake and his two brothers assumed someday they would too. Only his younger brother Bill had. Bill settled down in Denver and was the Theatre Arts Director at Denver University. His wife Sharon was Denver University's Affirmative Action Officer. Together they raised Jake's lovable godson, Luke. Jake's older brother Steven was an artist and a wanderer. Steven was presently living and painting in Brazil. Jake knew that Steven, like himself, was using his work as a distraction; both of them wanted what their parents and Bill already had.

Jake often wondered what his family would think of Jordon, assuming she weren't married. He decided they'd probably be put off at first by the age difference, but in no time they'd get past that and love her. After all, Jake thought, what's not to love?

Jake thought Jordon was remarkable in every way, but what he loved most about her was the ease with which they connected – on so many levels; Jake had never experienced that with anyone.

Jake began to sweat. He didn't know if it was because he was starting to run uphill or because he was thinking about her. His feelings for her sometimes overwhelmed him.

Before he met Jordon her reputation had preceded her. He'd heard she was very successful, smart, respectful of law enforcement, and gave one hundred percent to every case she worked on. He also knew she was married, had four kids, and was in her early 50s. He'd expected a frumpy middle-aged woman, but no such woman arrived; instead, he was greeted at the fire department by a youthful looking brunette with huge eyes, a great smile, and tight jeans.

When Jake first saw Jordon he had no idea who she was. She was simply talking to a fire-fighter, and Jake was drawn to her. Still, he remembered, it could have ended there. After all, he'd been attracted to other married women, but once he found out they were married, he lost interest; Jordon made that impossible.

Once Jake began working with her, he started to experience what a great listener she was, how much she cared about others, how zealous she felt about seeking justice, and how brave she was about stepping up and fighting for it. Jordon, he thought, had the poise and sexiness of a dancer, the brains of a scholar, and the protective passion of a mother. Jake didn't believe she was perfect, but he felt she was perfect for him, and he couldn't imagine ever loving anyone as much as he loved her. He also couldn't imagine Jordon ever breaking up her family.

Jake ran faster. He ended the run where he began, both mentally and physically, but at least now he was ready to be distracted by his mission to find Ming.

27

Sunday, April 6, 2006 8:00 a.m.

Stalking – Any person who willfully, maliciously, and repeatedly follows another person.

Muratoto remained parked outside Arty's hotel room until he emerged.

When Arty got into his car, Muratoto followed him.

At 11:43 a.m. Arty parked in front of Channel 7 and waited.

Muratoto waited too. I don't know what's going on, Muratoto thought, but at the very least I think he might be stalking her, but why?

28

Sunday, April 6, 2006 8:12 a.m.

Mens rea– Mind; intention; meaning; understanding; will

Jordon flinched as the sun's rays pierced the veil of her lashes.

"Damn, I slept in! I've got way too much to do to sleep in!" She sat up, looked around and realized it was after 8 o'clock: She hadn't slept that late in years. Why the hell haven't I gotten an update about my family? Or heard from Jake? She needed updates.

Jordon jumped out of bed and temporarily grayed-out. She sat back down. Low blood pressure, she thought, mixed with lack of food. Prioritize Danner - coffee, food, then get updates.

Jordon tried again: she stood up slowly and then carefully walked upstairs. Once in the kitchen she let the dogs out and re-filled their food bowls. A moment later she felt dizzy once more, so she sat back down.

"Okay, Danner," she said out loud, "take it easy." A moment later she went to the sink. Holding on to the sink, she grayed-out again. When she could see clearly, she drank a big glass of water. She knew there was nothing really wrong with her; she'd recently had a C.A.T. scan and multiple M.R.I.'s. She just worked too hard, they said, and worried too much, and sometimes forgot to eat in the process. First, she decided, make coffee. Then, toast a bagel. Finally, while both are in the works, get an update about my family.

The Officer who answered the phone told her he had nothing but good news to report. The weather had cleared up and he'd personally spoken to a spry Captain George who'd reported he was still confident they'd be in by 9 that night.

Jordon took a deep breath, thanked the officer, and hung up.

The room was filled with the aroma of brewing coffee and a toasting bagel. Jordon thought the smells were intoxicating, but then decided it was a bad choice of words. Today, she concluded, she'd have to make some final decisions about intoxicating agents; both her own and the one Diana consumed the night of her rape.

First hers; she called Jake's cell phone.

"This is Agent Manchester. I am temporarily unavailable. Please leave a message."

She loved hearing his voice, and resented the beep that followed.

"Good Morning Agent Manchester! This is District Attorney Danner, also known to you as JoJo. Where are you? Call me. Hope all is well." She paused for a moment, but added nothing.

Finally, Jordon was ready for her now-cold bagel and still-hot coffee. Her next call would be to the S.B.P.D. She wanted to see if any progress had been made in finding Dr. Swimmer's letter.

While she chewed her bagel, Jordon starred off in to the distance and wondered about West's *mens rea*.

Jordon concluded, West's *mens rea* was also her intoxicating agent. Maybe, she got off on watching the fire she created burn, but certainly, she was driven by hatred. Alexandra West hated the elderly, and she found it intoxicating to see them suffer.

29

Sunday, April 5, 2006 9 a.m.

"Tear Drop Tattoo" – A rudimentary tattoo injected in one inmate, by another; each tear symbolizing one completed year in state prison.

Jake arrived at Paradise Gardening at 9 o'clock. He didn't think anyone would be there on a Sunday morning, but hoped by just poking around he'd learn something about Ming. As soon as he drove up the gravel driveway a long haired German Shepherd started barking.

"Back off Bacara!" A burly middle aged man approached. "Sorry about the dog. He won't hurt you. He's honestly glad to see you. He likes visitors. Many of my customers bring him treats and he's probably just hoping you did too."

"No," Jake smiled, "I'm the worst kind of visitor; we've never met and I'm not bearing gifts."

"Well, I can take care of both those things." The man reached into his faded overall pocket, pulled out a piece of a dog biscuit, and gave it to Jake. Jake passed the morsel on to Bacara. "Okay," the man offered, "that takes care of the gift part - now on to the stranger part, I'm Steve Moran. I'm the owner of both this establishment and the wildebeest, Bacara." Steve returned Jake's smile.

"Good to meet you Steve. I'm Jake Manchester." Jake bent down and gave the now friendly dog a warm pat. "Bacara, that's an usual name for a dog - no?"

"Well, I've never met one. Bacara is the name of a local resort; it's just down the road. I did a considerable amount of work for them. They wanted the best of everything and their high standards gave me the dog of my dreams; thus, the name."

Steve scratched Bacara's behind his ears. In response, Bacara gave him a look of complete adoration. In a flash, Jake was envious and decided he wanted a dog.

"So," Steve continued, "if you haven't heard of The Bacara you must not be from around here."

"No, I'm not from around here, but I've been working a case here. I'm from Washington D.C. I work for the A.T.F." Jake handed Steve his card.

Steve looked shocked. He glanced at the card and again at Jake. His eyes widened as he pulled his head back. "The A.T.F.!" Steve smiled again. "Did one of my plants impersonate a tobacco leaf?"

Jake shook his head and laughed. "No, not that I know of, but would you mind if I ask you a couple of questions about one of your employees?"

Steve seemed surprised. "No, go ahead. But let's go talk down in my office. That way I'll be closer to my files."

Steve led the way. Jake was relieved Steve was being cooperative. Jake knew it would be tough to get a search warrant; he lacked probable cause and would have a heck of a time tracking down a judge on a Sunday. This, he thought, is much better.

They walked into the cluttered office. Steve poured Jake a cup of burnt-smelling coffee and they both sat down.

In the end, Jake found out Ming began working there about three years ago, having come from China via Texas. Steve figured, based on Ming's "tear-drop" tattoo, he'd served time in prison. Still, Steve wanted to give Ming a chance.

Over the years, Steve formed the opinion that Ming was a hard worker who mostly kept to himself. Although Steve never met Ming's family, Steve suspected Ming had a girlfriend who, when Ming was working in the office, occasionally called collect. Ming, Steve offered, always paid them back for those calls.

Jake cautiously told Steve he suspected the collect calls were from an arson-murderer presently incarcerated in the County Jail. Steve seemed shocked. He then compared the number on the phone bill to the one Jake gave him for the county jail. When they matched, Steve decided to open Ming's bolted locker. Inside, Steve found several of his stolen checks. He then offered to help Jake in any way he could.

When Jake asked for a list of Ming's customers, Steve hesitated at first, but after Jake assured him he just wanted to review the names, Steve printed it.

After looking over the list two names jumped out at Jake: Alexandra West and Marshall Riverstone. He'd heard Jordon mention the name Riverstone before, but he wasn't sure of the context. Jake decided to call Jordon as soon as he left Paradise.

30

Sunday, April 5, 2006 9:15 a.m.

Qui facitid quod plus est, facitid quod minus est, sed non convertitur – He who does that which is more, does that which is less, but not visa versa.

"Hey, you know I love you."

"Yes, Raul, I know you love me."

"And you know how you know I love you?'

"Yes, Raul, because you came in on a Sunday to look for evidence for me."

"And do you know how many other DAs I'd do that for?"

"One or two?"

"No, nada, none. You're it. And that's not because you're the D.A. It's because, ever since you were a baby D.A. you've busted your ass for us so I figured every now and then, I should do it for you, and you know why?"

Jordon was getting good at this. "Because you love me?"

"That's right Señora. Now, what the hell kind of letter am I looking for?"

Jordon explained she could fax him her faxed copy, but she needed the original.

Raul complained that there were hundreds of "miscellaneous pieces of paper" collected in the case, all of which had been thrown in multiple grocery-type bags. "It's gonna take me hours," Raul groaned, "but I'll do it."

"Can't you get someone to volunteer to help?" Jordon asked.

Raul began to sound exasperated. "Jordon, my dear, except for Saul, no one else besides me is allowed in the evidence room locker. Now, if you're done telling me how to do my job, I'll get off the phone and do it."

"Sorry, Raul," she offered. "Still love me?"

"Barely."

Jordon could hear him smile. "Okay, well, call me when you've got something to report. I won't bug you."

"You already have!"

Jordon could hear him chortle.

As soon as Jordon hung up she called Tuttini's, her favorite bakery, and asked them to deliver a basket of their most scrumptious treats to Raul at the Santa Barbara Police Department. Jordon also told them to include a note: "With love from your favorite pain in the ass." When she dictated the note to Susan, Tuttini's owner, they both laughed.

As soon as Jordon put the phone down, Jake called.

"Who," he asked without formality, "is Marshall Riverstone?"

"The worst!" Jordon felt as if she'd been kicked in the solar plexus.

"Well I was going to ask friend or foe, but I think I already got my answer."

"He's the child pornographer we've been watching on and off for the last couple of years."

"You've been watching him, huh? So tell me, who's his gardener?"

"His gardener?" Jordon asked. "Oh shit, don't tell me, it's Ming!"

"None other."

"So, do you think there's some sort of a connection?"

"Don't know, but I intend to find out."

"How?"

"Well, let's start with what we already know. Tell me about this guy."

Jordon told Jake about Marshall Riverstone, or as she kept referring to him, "the snake who slithered away."

"As I said, Marshall Riverstone is a child pornographer," Jordon had a discernible lump in her throat, "and probably a drug dealer. I was prosecuting him a couple of years ago and he got off on a technicality, not once, but twice. And to add insult to injury, he actually donated ten thousand dollars to my campaign. Well, I took that ten thousand and instantly put it in a separate account for use at some later date to hire an expert to help me successfully prosecute the snake the next time he got caught." Jordon took a deep breath. "But ever since Riverstone gave me that money, he's been slithering under the radar."

"Maybe," Jake replied.

"What do you mean maybe?"

"Well, you know I function as if there are no coincidences."

"Have you talked to Ming yet?"

"No, first I have to get as much information as I can about Riverstone and Ming individually, before I approach either one of them to figure out if there is a connection.

Ming's boss said Ming was out of town for the day so I thought I'd check out Riverstone first. Who was your go-to detective on Riverstone's case?"

"Well, he wasn't a detective, he was a patrol officer. Actually, he was a great cop who got a bum rap because Riverstone bought himself a sleazy defense attorney who sold a malleable judge on the idea that Officer Howe behaved unethically."

"What? What happened?"

"It's a long story but the bottom line is the cop's name is Paul Howe and there's nothing he'd rather do than nail Riverstone."

"But would he rather do that than hang out with his friends and family on a Sunday?"

"Yep."

"Okay, I'll give him a call. This is getting better and better. So how're you doing?"

Jordon told him about the search for the letter and her latest thoughts on <u>Cantera</u>.

***

Jake became very excited about Raul coming in, but uncomfortable with Raul teasing Jordon by saying he loved her. Even when Jake heard Raul was 10 years past his retirement age, his concern didn't entirely disappear. "Jordon," he asked, "what is it with you and men in law enforcement?"

"Believe me: it's not me, it's them; they are starved for female companionship."

"Hardly!" Jake said, "Telling a woman I'm an A.T.F. agent is the best *chick magnet* I have."

As soon as Jake used those words, with that tone, he was sorry. He knew Jordon hated the word 'chick' for woman and he never wanted her to feel as if she had any competition. As far as he was concerned, she didn't, and he feared if she felt she did, she'd throw up her hands and walk away. The fact of the matter was he had women, and chicks, throwing themselves at him all the time, but compared to her, they just seemed like cardboard cut-outs.

***

Jake's words stung. Picturing other women flirting with him always left Jordon feeling foolish and vulnerable. She knew how gorgeous he was and never could figure out why he was romantically interested in her. There are so many young, beautiful, and single women who'd jump at the chance to be with him. Why should I keep this ridiculous charade going? "Jake…"

"Jordon," he immediately cut her off. "I'm sorry, I apologize, I should never have said that."

"But Jake, it's true. We both know–"

"JoJo, how 'bout we don't talk about what *we both know* at the moment and just talk about what we have to do, we're up against a clock."

Jordon knew he was right; the problem was she was up against too many clocks.

"Look," he continued, "I'll call you later with whatever I find out. What time do you think you'll be heading home?"

"Probably around five."

"Okay, so how 'bout we meet for dinner at seven?"

Jordon was expecting her family no earlier than 9 o'clock, so 7 o'clock would work.

Now, as she thought about sitting across a table from him in just a matter of hours, she felt herself flush. "Seven's great. Joe's?" she asked. They both loved Joe's and spent many evenings there nursing 'Old Fashions' while working into the early morning hours.

* * *

"Joe's is perfect." Jake smiled. He was glad she chose what he considered to be 'their place.' He took it as a positive sign. "Meanwhile, I'm going to pursue this Ming-Riverstone connection and call you if, or when, anything comes up. If you don't hear from me it'll probably be because I'm running with something, but I will call you if I'm going to be late."

As soon as they hung up Jake called the Police Department dispatcher, who put him through to Paul Howe's home.

Just as Jordon predicted, Howe couldn't wait to get involved. He showed up at The Daily Ground, a local coffee House, twenty-three minutes after Jake called.

* * *

Jake and Paul sat at a corner table.

As their waitress approached, she noticed they were both unusually handsome and sexy. She tightened her apron and fixed her hair; even she knew there was no hiding her exuberance.

"Good morning Gentlemen! My name is Gracie; I'll be your server this morning."

For a moment they ignored her, seemingly focused on their animated conversation. Then they looked up and gave her warm, but non-flirtatious, smiles. Gracie quickly surmised they were accustomed to getting appreciative looks from woman, and although neither of them appeared rude, they also didn't seem interested.

Gracie stood by as they studied the menu. The blonde guy, Gracie noted, was wearing a tee-shirt which indicated his name was Paul, and he coached a girl's water polo team named The Dolphins. Okay Gracie thought, he coaches now but I'll bet anyone he played water polo in college and still works out. His shirt fits him perfectly, except for being slightly tight around the biceps. Gracie eyed his arms right down to his hands and saw his well-buffed wedding ring. Paul, Gracie concluded, is happily married and I'll bet he even has a beautiful long-legged daughter who's the star player on The Dolphins.

Next, Gracie turned her attention to the other guy. Hmm, she thought, half white, and one hundred percent stunning. Gracie noticed he was wearing a tan button down shirt with subtle light blue stripes. The shirt's colors, she observed, almost perfectly matched his skin tone and eyes. His top button was open and his sleeves rolled up. Gracie wanted to see what was beyond that top button.

Gracie still hadn't left her location next to the table, and hoped she appeared professional and responsive, but assumed she looked as captivated as she felt. A moment later, she dropped her head slightly as if to suggest she was searching for her small pad, when in reality, she was still gawking at their arms. Gracie had always thought a man's arms were among the sexiest parts of his body.

***

After amiably consulting with Gracie, Paul and Jake ordered their breakfast. Each had come to learn it's always best to befriend members of the public, since one never knew when they might be needed.

After Gracie walked away, beaming, they turned their attention back to Riverstone.

Jake decided he would go undercover by impersonating a newly immigrated Jamaican gardener, a temporary replacement for Ming. He would go to Riverstone's house in a van from Paradise, and Paul would hide in the back of the van. Of course, they'd have to get Steve's permission, but Jake felt confident once he divulged Riverstone's past, Steve would give it.

***

As they pulled away from the coffee shop, unbeknownst to them, Gracie went running after the van. Two blocks later Jake saw her, stopped, and got out of the car. Gracie gave him his cell phone and a breathless explanation, "The, the clip must've broken; you, you left it behind." Jake handed the phone to Paul, then he offered Gracie heartfelt thanks and a hug; Gracie readily accepted both.

After driving Gracie back to the restaurant, they were once again on their way.

***

An hour later, Jake and Paul were going up a long driveway in Santa Ynez, an exclusive section of Northern Santa Barbara County. As they crested the incline, they saw, in the distance, a white plantation-style mansion. The manor was surrounded by a closely cropped lawn the size of a small golf course.

"I guess there's lots of money to be made in child pornography," Jake sneered.

"Don't get me started, Jake," Paul mumbled from his hiding place in the back. "Jordon has already chastised me for losing my objectivity once with this guy and it would take very little for me to do it again. I owe it to Jordon not to fuck this one up. She's a helluva D.A."

Jake merely nodded. He felt both proud and a little bit jealous at the same time.

Several yards away from the entrance, Jake spotted the words RIVERSTONE in large brass letters prominently displayed on an ornate wrought-iron gate. Less obviously exhibited, were several video cameras and a small callbox.

Jake smiled for one of the cameras as he pushed a button on the callbox.

"May I help you?" The voice said, sounding anything but solicitous.

"Paradise Garden'n." Jake said in a near-flawless Jamaican accent.

"But where's Ming?" A now confused-sounding male voice responded.

"Me a Ming fren, him send me because him tell me when him here last time one of de roses no look good. An him send me, me a rose trimma man."

There was silence on the other end. "Well, it would be better if you came back tomorrow with Ming."

Jake would not be turned away. "Monday no good man. Me a work Monday an Tuesday. Me haf ta look on de roses tiday." Jake and Paul both held their breath; they knew they didn't have any reason to get a warrant and this scam was the best they could come up with on such short notice.

"Well, alright then, but you know Ming never told me he was concerned about the roses. I'll wait for you in front of the house and you can show me which rose bush Ming mentioned."

There was another long pause, as if the speaker were still deciding whether to admit him.

Finally, the buzzer sounded, Jake exhaled, and drove in.

As soon as Jake pulled in, he saw Riverstone was waiting. He thought Riverstone appeared immaculately groomed, and seemed strangely uncomfortable.

Jake got out of the van, left the driver's door open, and stayed close by. Even though Jake was wired, he wanted to be sure Paul could hear everything that was said. Jake looked around and pointed to a distant clump of rose bushes claiming they looked distressed.

Riverstone seemed less interested in the roses, and more concerned about Ming's whereabouts. "So where's Ming today?" he asked while running his perfectly manicured nails through his thick grey hair. "I mean, how come he didn't come with you?" Riverstone was obviously trying to keep his inquiry sounding casual.

"Yeah," answered Jake, "I aks Ming same thing. I mean we is fren, but if I got to work on a Sunday I got to know why him not by me side."

"Well, maybe we should call him up. Do you have his home number?"

"He not home now; him tell me him own self." Jake began to worry, but took comfort in the fact that Riverstone didn't know how to reach Ming, at least for the time being.

"Well, where did he go?"

"Him no tell me man, him just say it was important and him heading out of town all day." Jake was glad Steve had mentioned that.

"So," Riverstone asked, "Ming said it was *important* and he was going out of town, but he didn't say anything else?"

Jake shook his head no.

Riverstone started looking around; he was clearly becoming increasingly anxious. A moment later he invited Jake into the house; Jake followed him.

Once in the living room, Riverstone offered Jake a drink; Jake refused. Riverstone poured himself a Scotch and chugged it. Soon, Riverstone seemed to have forgotten Jake was there.

Jake didn't disturb him. Instead he just watched as Riverstone stood perfectly still, except for repeatedly running his fingers through his hair.

Suddenly, Riverstone began to pace; soon sweat appeared on his temples.

"Listen," Riverstone said, stopping in front of a vast window. "You've got to help me find Ming." Riverstone looked right into Jake's eyes. "You understand? You find me Ming and I give you a thousand dollars."

Jake stared right back at him. Jake had learned a long time ago that being silent, in certain circumstances, can be extremely useful.

"Okay," Riverstone said, "I'll make it five thousand, but it's got to be today."

31

Sunday April 5, 2006 11:00 a.m.

Deceit – The act of intentionally giving a false impression.

Jordon wondered how things were going with Jake's search for Ming. She tried Jake's cell phone again, but when he didn't answer, she called Paradise Gardening directly. Jordon made the call on a whim; she felt out of control and wanted to know where Jake was.

Steve answered, "Paradise Gardening. Steve speaking."

"Good morning. Is Ming there?"

"Ming Ong?"

Jordon hesitated; she now realized she had no idea what Ming's last name was. "I'm sorry, I don't know Ming's last name; he does gardening for a friend of mine and she asked me to leave him a message about her hedge." Jordon was fabricating her story as she went along.

Steve hesitated, "Well, Ming Ong's a gardener who, err, works... worked... for me but, who are you?"

Jordon was at a loss for words. "Err; just tell him the hedge needs trimming." Then she hung up.

Jordon felt like a fool. What, she wondered, did she now have that she didn't have before she placed the call? Beyond that, she might have endangered Jake by sounding like an idiot and perhaps tipping off Steve, whoever the hell he was. And still she didn't know where Jake was. All she had was Ming the gardener's last name, but she had no idea where he fit in, if in fact he fit in at all. Who the hell is Ming?

Jordon walked back out to the front porch. And who is he to Riverstone? More importantly, who is he to

Alexandra? Just a gardener? But he called a few times - perhaps a friend? Lover? Accomplice? Well, not that, because Ruthie's neighbor Judge Patel saw only Alexandra come out of the rental van. The rental van! Shit, she thought, the rental van; the one we've never been able to trace because we had only Alexandra's name. Where did Patel think that van came from? She'd have to check her notes.

Jordon went running downstairs. Oh my God, she froze; Ming even mentioned a van in his taped call to Alexandra. Why the hell didn't Jordon think of this before?

She dove into the box, found the report containing Patel's interview, and quickly perused it. "Budget!" She said out loud.

Jordon called Information for Budget's Santa Barbara office. This time she had a plan before she spoke.

"Budget Rent-A-Car; Molly speaking. How may we serve you?"

Jordon thought Molly sounded just like the kind of voice she'd hoped to hear.

"Yes, well, hi," Jordon began slowly, "I'd like to rent a van."

"Well sure," the sweet young voice chorused, "I can help you with that; if not at our own branch, through any other of our branches in the Tri-County region. What kind of van are you looking for?"

"Ah, this is going to sound kinda silly, you see I'm actually looking for a *certain* older van."

"A certain van?"

"I'm sorry," Jordon offered, "I don't mean to sound weird. Molly, do you have a minute for me to try and explain to you what's *really* going on?"

"Well, yeah."

Molly now seemed intrigued, just what Jordon was hoping for. Jordon's voice became wistful as she explained that on Sunday, August 17, 2004, her then fiancé, Ming Ong, rented a van, took her up into the mountains, and asked her to marry him. She of course, said yes. Then to seal their promise they became "intimate" in the van. "It was the best moment of my life," Jordon offered. "Next Friday," Jordon continued, "will be our wedding anniversary, and I thought it would be really cool to get the same van. Maybe this time, we might actually make a baby, you see we've been trying, and it just hasn't worked out–"

"Oh, I'm sorry," Molly interrupted.

Jordon could tell she practically had the young clerk in tears.

Jordon felt badly about being disingenuous, especially about such a sensitive topic, but she knew it was all for a good cause.

Within a matter of moments, Molly promised Jordon she'd do everything she could to figure out which van it was. "It's probably gonna take me at least an hour to run his name, and we probably won't still have that exact van in our fleet," Molly paused, "but I'll give it my all. Why don't you just give me your number and I'll call you back."

Bingo, Jordon thought. "That is so sweet of you, Molly."

Before hanging up, Jordon gave Molly her telephone number and sincere thanks.

Jordon was now waiting for multiple calls: updates from her family and Jake, as well as return calls from Raul and Molly. She decided she shouldn't leave the house to go for a run; she put on a leotard, grabbed a collection of Motown tunes, and got on her exercise bike. After peddling for five minutes, Jordon jumped off the bike to answer the ringing phone.

"Hello?" Jordon was careful not to say her name in case it was Molly calling back sooner than expected.

"Mrs. Danner?"

Jordon heard police radio noise in the background. "Yes, this is Jordon Danner. What's going on?" The voice on the other end of the phone sounded serious; Jordon feared the call had something to do with her family.

"Mrs. Danner. This is Officer Page from the Coast Guard." Jordon held her breath. "We just got word from your son that the repair job is taking longer than expected and that they have changed their E.T.A. to midnight because they probably won't be getting off the island until sunset."

Jordon quietly exhaled, "Are they okay?"

"Yes, George assured me they are, he just wants to give the patching extra time to dry. He said he and your husband were continuing to do minor repairs and your younger son Sam was still trying to spear a calico bass for you."

Jordon's eyes reddened.

"Ma'am," Page continued, "George sounded good and he told me to tell you not to worry."

"Okay, thank you Officer, but tell me - what do you think? Do you think there's a problem? Do you think they are safe leaving so late? Do you think I'm just being a crazy paranoid wife and mother?"

"I'll answer the last question first. I think you are being a wonderful wife and mother."

Not so, she thought.

"And," Page continued, "given your son's reputation, and the good weather ahead, I think they'll be just fine."

Why, Jordon wondered do these calls from the Coast Guard take me on such an emotional roller-coaster? It must be the guilt, she concluded. "Thank you," she told Page, "and I should be at this number until about 5:00, after that, if anything else comes up, you can reach me on my cell." Jordon paused. "Please tell my boys I'll be waiting up for them at home."

"No problem ma'am, and I still have that cell number so don't you worry. I'll call you if I need to; you just have yourself a safe trip home."

Jordon felt relieved. She returned to the stationary bike and pulled herself back on. Sly and the Family Stone were singing: "I want to take you higher..." Jordon sang along and started to become light-hearted. Soon, she realized her newfound joy was not only because she was told her family remained safe, but also because she'd now have more time with Jake at dinner. Jordon stopped singing and peddled harder.

Next came The Supremes, who relentlessly sang: "Ain't no mountain high enough..." Jordon couldn't wait until she sat across the candlelit table from Jake. She had to be honest, at least with herself: she loved Greg, but she had fallen in-love with Jake. If it were just she and Greg maybe she'd tell Greg she needed a break to sort things out, but there were also the boys. But they, she argued back, are grown up and I owe it to myself, and Jake, to see what's what; I mean, you only live once and if Jake is my true love - how can I cast him aside? I can't, but I should: my first allegiance is to my kids, and Sam is not fully grown, he's just a junior in high school. Maybe I could just ask Jake to wait until Sam has gone off to college. I mean, I owe it to Sam, I brought him into this world I can't screw it up for him. I've got to stay for Sam's sake.

She kept peddling. The Temptations started singing "I wish it would rain..." Jordon became teary.

Jordon got off the bike 45 minutes later, soaked with sweat and still mentally repeating - she had to 'stay for Sam's sake.'

As Jordon showered, she began to think that what she really had to do for 'Sam's sake' was to follow her heart. If Sam were married, she imagined, and through no fault of his own, he fell in love with someone else, Jordon would want him to examine, and then follow, his heart. True love, Jordon rationalized, is too precious and rare to be cast aside.

For Sam's sake...she thought.

For Sam's sake, perhaps I should be brave and follow my heart.

Jordon knew it wasn't going to be easy and she hated herself for falling in love with Jake, but she had to be a real, not fictitious, role model for Sam, his brothers, and the truth. And Greg, she continued to ruminate, he'd find someone else; he was too wonderful a man not to.

Jordon felt both guilty and energized by her latest thought; it was the first time she'd given any real consideration to spending the rest of her life with Jake.

A few minutes later the phone rang again.

"Hello?"

"Danner? Who loves you, baby?"

"You do Raul."

"And how do you know I love you?"

"Because you came in on a Sunday just to look for my letter?"

"No, my dear, because I came in on a Sunday and *found* your letter! It was inside another letter in a totally different envelope."

"Raul - you are the best!"

As soon as Jordon set the phone down, it rang again.

"Hellooo" Jordon kept her voice wistful, thinking it might be Molly from Budget.

"Yes, this is Molly from Budget Rent a Car. Is this Mrs. err, Ong?"

Jordon didn't want to lie, so she didn't answer Molly's question. "Oh, hi Molly," she responded, "did you find the van Ming rented?"

"Well, actually, I've got bad news for you."

Jordon was disappointed. She had hoped she'd found another piece of the puzzle. "So, what's the bad news?" she asked.

"We don't have *that* van anymore, we sold it."

Jordon couldn't believe her good luck. "But you are sure he rented that van from you on August seventeenth, two thousand and four?"

"Oh, quite sure, I have the paperwork right in front of me…Ming Ong…he actually rented it on August sixteenth and then returned it late at night on August seventeenth. But gosh, I'm so sorry I couldn't have been more helpful."

Jordon wished there was a way to tell Molly she'd been incredibly helpful, but Jordon didn't want to blow her cover. "Molly, you've been terrific. Just one last thing, could you make me a copy of that paperwork? I'd like to keep it as a–"

"Oh, I totally understand." Molly sounded bubbly again. "I'll just make a copy for you now. Would you like me to mail it to you at the address Mr. Ong listed?"

Oh God no, thought Jordon. "No, no thank-you," she said, "I'd like to surprise him. Can I just have someone pick it up there tomorrow?"

"Oh sure, absolutely, you know what they say…'anything for love!'"

Jordon smiled and thanked her again. First thing Monday morning, Jordon decided, she'd have an investigator pick up Molly's copy. Then she'd have Budget Headquarters served with the subpoena. Jordon couldn't wait to tell Jake what happened, but she'd have to wait: Jake said he'd be running around and would call her if he could. Still, since she was on a roll, maybe she'd just go ahead and call Diana.

Jordon knew Diana worked in her office Sunday afternoon to prepare for their Monday interviews. Jordon got up, went over to the <u>Cantera</u> file, and found Diana's office number.

"Diana Johnson here!"

"Hi Diana, Jordon Danner here."

There was no response. Jordon sensed as soon as Diana realized who the caller was, she felt deflated.

***

Diana was working on interview questions for a guest author when suddenly the phone rang; it was the D.A. from Santa Barbara. Diana liked Jordon, but she didn't want to talk to her; Diana just wanted the whole thing to go away. She wanted her rapist convicted, but she didn't want to testify. She dreaded telling the jury about how much she'd had to drink and that she remembered nothing. She already felt like an idiot for what she'd done and feared that saying it out loud to a bunch of strangers would only make things worse. Beyond that, she still didn't know what her rapist looked like and was afraid seeing him in court would really rock her. Diana wanted to drop the charges, but she also didn't want anyone else to go through the hell she'd been through. She hoped Jordon was calling to say the guy was going to plead guilty, but Diana knew that wasn't likely. Jordon already told Diana the evidence was shaky and her rapist had a nasty lawyer. Jordon had also made it clear that even after Diana suffered through testifying, for perhaps days, the jury might still disbelieve her and find him not guilty. Nevertheless, Diana felt she had to do everything she could to protect his next potential victim, and so she planned on going through with it.

"Hey Jordon," she finally responded, "good news? Bad news? Or more questions?"

"All of the above."

Jordon explained to Diana the state of the case. After that, she began to introduce the concepts of blackouts and alcoholism. Diana listened and soon began to weep.

32

Sunday, April 5, 2006 12:15 p.m.

Miranda Admonishment – The warnings suspects who have been placed in custody must be given before they can be questioned regarding the alleged crime.

Jake decided watching and listening to Riverstone rant on about Ming's dangerous and unpredictable nature was, at the moment, better than questioning him. What's more, if a *Miranda* issue came up later, Jake could always play the tape Howe was now making, which would prove Riverstone spoke to Jake without being placed in custody or questioned, and therefore Jake had not violated *Miranda*.

"You've got to find him." Riverstone said, as he continued to pace while Jake continued to watch and listen.

"Don't you understand? Your friend, your *fren*, could be in a lot of trouble. I could be in a lot of trouble too - it could be a matter of life and death!"

That's it, Jake thought. "Sit down, Mr. Riverstone." Jake's Jamaican accent was gone.

Marshall Riverstone stopped pacing. He turned quickly to face Jake as if to make sure those words came from his mouth. Riverstone's eyes widen. "What the fuck?"

Jake repeated himself, "Sit down, Mr. Riverstone."

Marshall Riverstone slowly sat down. Once he was seated, Jake began to speak. Jake explained who he was, what information he was seeking, and then gave Riverstone his *Miranda* warnings.

Riverstone, being no novice to police investigations and legal loopholes, told Jake he was ready to talk, but first he wanted *absolute* immunity, or at least *use* immunity.

"Bottom line, I don't want you guys using my statements against me."

Jake wasn't about to offer Riverstone any kind of immunity, whether he legally could or not, unless he understood what Riverstone's level of culpability was.

***

Riverstone knew he had to give the A.T.F. agent enough to get the promise of immunity, but not so much that if decided not to give him immunity, or if they gathered evidence from other sources, his statements wouldn't incriminate him. In a flash Riverstone thought back to a moment almost 30 years ago when he briefly attended architecture school.

The instructor told the class to build a bridge out of sticks. The bridge was to be strong enough to support one brick, but collapse when two bricks were placed upon it. Riverstone was the only student to successfully complete the task; most of the other student's bridges didn't collapse when the second brick was added.

Not too much information, Riverstone cautioned himself, just enough, just one brick.

"Let's hear it Riverstone," Jake growled, "I'm not a patient man, especially when it comes to life and death."

Riverstone sat down and once again ran his hand past his now sweaty forehead and through his damp hair. "What," he began slowly, "if I gave you information that saved someone from being murdered and you later decided that maybe I had something to do with those plans."

Jake walked over to Riverstone, grabbed him by the outside of his shoulders, and lifted him up. Their faces were no more than 3 inches apart. Jake snarled, "*If* your timely information saves someone's life, you got your *use* immunity; if not, you and I both know the D.A. who will take great pleasure in frying you."

Jake let go and Riverstone collapsed back down onto the couch.

"Not to mention the cop." Paul Howe walked in. Riverstone sat up; his face was plastered with panic. "Now asshole," Howe ordered, "start talking."

The moment Marshall Riverstone saw Paul Howe walk in, Riverstone felt devastated; he'd finally given Howe the moment he'd been waiting for.

Five years ago Riverstone humiliated Howe by having a lawyer insinuate Howe had misused his police powers, although Howe and Riverstone both knew he hadn't. Still, Riverstone was sure Howe had spent the last five years defending himself against Riverstone's lawyer's bogus claims. Throughout those five years Howe made sure Riverstone thought Howe was watching him – just seeking justice. But Riverstone was no fool; he knew Howe was seeking revenge.

***

Paul Howe hated Marshall Riverstone. Paul had met some of the child actors and models featured in Riverstone's pornography. Truth be known, Paul enjoyed seeing Riverstone cower. You, you son of a bitch, Paul thought, were in control then, but I'm in control now.

***

Jake saw the gleam in Paul's eyes. Jake would let Paul interrogate Riverstone, but not if he delayed Jake from getting word to the vulnerable victim, whoever he or she was. Jake pulled over a chair for Paul.

"Okay," Paul told Riverstone "you've got your use immunity. We won't *use* your statements against you, but I'm not going to give you 'absolute.' If we can prove your involvement without your words, you'll still be on the hook. Now if you don't start talking fast you'll lose the - use."

"Well," Riverstone began, "Ming's my gardener, but you know that. Friday was an exceedingly hot day. He was watering the plants on the porch. I brought him a glass of water and left the screen door open."

Riverstone seemed to be gaining some of his arrogance back.

"The sunroom TV was on. While Ming drank, he looked over at the TV. That Darcy Danielson was reporting the <u>West</u> jury had hung. Right after that, the camera panned to Jordon Danner's miserable face. That was when Ming began to laugh. Then, still staring at the TV, he snarled, 'Bitch!' 'Who,' I asked, 'Darcy Danielson?"' Ming appeared taken aback. 'Nah,' he said, 'I was talking about the D.A.' Then he asked me if I knew her. That's when I told him she once tried to frame me, but failed. Then Ming said that West was also one of his customers and he was glad Danner failed again. That's when I got out the tequila, invited him in, and we started toasting to Danner's failures. After about an hour, Ming admitted West was actually his girlfriend and I acknowledged Danner was still hassling me. After another hour and 3 more shots of tequila, Ming told me that if Danner dropped the case against his girlfriend, she could fight her aunt's will and maybe they'd get some money. Then I told him if Danner dropped dead, my life would be a whole lot easier."

Jake stood up. In that instant, it became clear to him who the vulnerable victim was. Jake and Paul exchanged a knowing look and Jake sprinted to their van.

33

Sunday, April 5, 2006 12:30 p.m.

Conspiracy to Commit Murder – An agreement between two or more persons to commit an unlawful homicide.

Jordon heard the silencing click of her call-waiting, but decided not to interrupt her conversation with Diana. Jordon feared if she got off the line now, Diana wouldn't be there when Jordon returned, and instead would start drinking. The call-waiting-click continued. This caller, Jordon thought, is persistent; maybe it's about my family. Jordon asked Diana to hang on for a moment and pressed "FLASH".

"Hello?" Jordon thought she heard someone breathe. She said 'hello' again. They hung up. Damn hang ups, she thought.

"Diana, I'm sorry – it was just another hang-up, my second one today. I won't interrupt our call again; I promise. So how are you doing with all this?"

***

Perfect, the caller thought.

***

As soon Jake opened the van door, he saw his cell phone on the seat and once again appreciated Gracie's kindness. He pressed "Jordon." When Jordon didn't pick up on the third ring he began to pray. A moment later he was cursing.

Although he had directions to Jordon's mountain cabin, he had no idea what county she was in or who the closest law enforcement agency was. He decided to start driving and use his cell phone to sort it all out. First he called S.B.P.D. dispatch to secure back-up for Howe, then he tried to call Jordon, but Jordan didn't answered and the phone ran incessantly. Jake allowed his anger to swell; it helped to temper his growing sense of panic. Where the hell are you, Jordon?

Jake's next call was to the Highway Patrol. Jake asked to speak with an officer who was familiar with the thoroughfares leading up to the mountain roads near Mount Able.

Jake was connected to Officer Chris Valentine. Jake identified himself, told Valentine what was going on, and who Jake feared was in danger. Unbeknownst to Jake, Chris Valentine and Jordon had started out their careers together.

***

Chris was taken aback, but at the same time he was glad it was he who took the A.T.F. agent's call.

"Valentine," Jake asked, "are you still there?"

"Yeah, I'm sorry. It's just that Jordon and I go way back."

"Great, then we're on the same page: Jordon and I are friends too, so, let's not let that son of a bitch get her. I'm gonna give you the directions she gave me, then you tell me which agency can get to her first."

Jake's directions helped Chris quickly surmise that the nearest law enforcement agency was an hour away. A helicopter might be able to get there in half that time, but it might also spook Ming and that was the last thing they wanted to do.

***

Jordon heard the call waiting clicks again but she refused to be interrupted by another hang-up call; especially now when she could sense Diana was just beginning to understand.

"Jordon," Diana asked, her voice almost a whisper, "do *you* think I'm an alcoholic?"

"Diana, I can't answer that. And you should know, I have prosecuted many of these kinds of cases where the women were legally intoxicated, maybe even blacked-out, but they weren't alcoholics."

Jordon paused before continuing.

"Diana, bottom line: only you know how much you drink and how dependant you are upon it. But you've told me your dad is an alcoholic and I'm sure you know this can be passed on either genetically or environmentally. And I know its one thing for you to consider the issue as it relates to you and another for you to go public with it."

"Public?"

"Well, yeah, for us to ask the jury to consider that you experienced a black-out, and that's why you can't remember the assailant or the assault, you pretty much have to admit, on the stand, that you have an issue with alcohol."

"Whoah, I can't do that. Even though the media can't use my name, somehow news of this could make its way up here to my bosses and they'll never promote me. Hell, they may even fire me. Listen, I told you right from the beginning," Diana's voice was becoming loud and accusatory. "I didn't want anyone up here to find out, that's why I wouldn't let you publicize my picture in order to find people who might have seen him walk away with me. I know it would have helped our case if one of them would've seen us and seen how out of it I was, but I…"

Jordon could hear the agony in Diana's voice.

"I, I," Diana continued, "told you I couldn't do that, and now, now you're asking me to do so much more. You're asking me to admit to the world that I'm a drunk. Well, I won't, I'm sorry, Jordon. I can't. I won't…"

Jordon could hear Diana sob. She wanted to let Diana cry it out; she just hoped Diana wouldn't hang up. And still, Jordon thought, those damn call waiting signals keep interrupting us; no way I'm getting off this call again.

"Diana," Jordon said, "I'm right here with you."

***

"Jake, where are you now?" CHP Officer Chris Valentine asked.

"Just passing Cayumas."

Chris was pacing. He'd already contacted Santa Barbara, Ventura, and Kern County Sheriffs Department. They were all very responsive; after all, who wouldn't want to be the hero agency that saved the well-liked D.A.? Unfortunately, Chris wasn't convinced any of them could get there more quickly than Jake could.

"So where does that put us?" Jake asked.

"Looks like you, and almost everybody else, are about thirty-eight minutes away."

"Fuck!" Jake snarled as he hit his steering wheel with his sweaty fist.

Chris paused for a moment before asking him again, "Do you want to re-consider the helicopter?"

"No. Do you?"

Chris couldn't tell if Jake was really asking his opinion or just barking at him. One thing Chris was sure of, Jake was extremely upset. Chris wondered just how close Jake and Jordon really were. Chris exhaled and then answered, "No, I agree with you."

There was silence on the line.

"Valentine, are your people *continuously* trying to call her?" Jake sounded accusatory.

"As often as I direct them to." Chris replied.

"What do you mean by that?" Jake clearly wanted someone constantly pressing redial.

Chris was now convinced Jake was, in some way, emotionally involved with Jordon. Jake wanted them to call constantly, but Chris knew that wasn't a good idea. Everyone in law enforcement had been taught if a hostage taker heard a phone ring too much, he'd think someone was onto him, and he'd kill his hostage, therefore, protocol dictated infrequent calls only. Jake, Chris decided, is too close. But, Chris worried, what if she isn't being held hostage, and hasn't even been approached yet? Then, the phone call could warn her. Still, in situations like this, it's just best to stick with the protocol.

"Agent Manchester…" Chris started off cautiously.

"It's Jake."

"Fair enough, Jake, I read the papers. I know you just got off a big case with her; I've done that, she's awesome, but–"

"The best!" Jake responded. Chris could hear the crack in Jake's voice.

"Yeah, the best, and knowing that's how you feel, maybe you're too close to make the calls. Why don't you concentrate on getting there as fast as you can, and trust me to handle *intel* until you do."

***

Jake knew Chris was right, but letting go had never been one of Jake's strengths. Jake swallowed down the tightness in his throat. "Okay Valentine – that makes sense. I'm going to hang up now. You call her as often as you think you should and I'll call you when I'm ten minutes away. Meanwhile, call me if any of the others are any closer or if you get through to her. For now, I'll just plan on hiding my car and hiking in the last piece. Unless you think–"

"No, that's fine, anyway you're about to lose cell service. Meanwhile, I'll get some maps out to help with your final approach. We'll talk soon. Drive safe."

"Yeah," Jake said, "and thanks."

Jake put down his phone and concentrated on the road ahead. Soon he was gritting his teeth and wiping his face with the back of his hand. If only, he thought, I'd pursued the Ming angle first, and then maybe I could've stopped this before it began.

***

Jordon heard the sound of a car coming up her gravel road.

"Diana, can you hang on for just a second? I think someone's here. Will you hang on or should I just call you back?"

Diana didn't answer. Jordon didn't want to risk interrupting their call; she still feared Diana would start drinking or worse. "Never mind, I'll just take the phone outside with me." As Jordon walked toward her front door she took a deep breath and asked, "Diana, what's your worst fear? That you'll lose face? Your job? Friends? Family? Or…that you'll have to stop the closet drinking?" Jordon hope she hadn't gone too far, that she wasn't being, "brutally honest," again.

There was no immediate answer.

"I don't know," Diana finally responded, "it all sounds pretty scary, and now maybe I don't want to. I mean if we never went to trial I could deal with this privately and he'd–"

"Win," Jordon interrupted, "and get away with raping you." Ooh, Jordon thought, brutally honest. Still, I better let that thought sink in.

Jordon stepped outside and saw a truck pull into her driveway.

***

Jake answered after the first ring. "Did you reach her?" Jake assumed it was Chris.

"Jake, its Paul. I'm still up here at Riverstone's. I'm sure you figured it all out by now, but I just got confirmation. Riverstone and Ming ended up talking for quite a long time, and based upon a message Ming left him, Riverstone thinks Ming actually believes Riverstone hired him to kill Jordon. And he thinks Ming might be at Jordon's place now."

It hurt to hear Paul say "kill Jordon" and "now." Jake and Valentine had thus far avoided using those words.

"Jake, are you still there?" Paul asked.

"Yeah, I'm here and that's what I figured." Jake cleared his throat. "That's why I left in such a hurry. I'm trying to get to her, but she's not answering the phone."

"Jake, look, everything's okay here. Thanks for sending the backup. Riverstone is still *spilling*. You just focus on saving our girl and I'll get whatever details I can out of this piece of shit."

Paul hung up before Jake could tell him to give Riverstone absolute immunity in exchange for any information that might save Jordon. Jake considered calling Paul back, but concluded it was unlikely an A.T.F. agent would have authority to offer absolute immunity; Jake doubted he even had authority to grant him use immunity, but he did it anyhow.

The phone rang again. Jake thought it might be Paul wanting to discuss Riverstone's immunity.

"Paul?"

"No, it's Chris."

"Chris, did you reach her?"

"No," he answered, sounding as disappointed as he knew Jake felt. "The line's still ringing. Listen Kern County Sheriff's Department is fifteen minutes away and asking me what they should do next. Where are you?"

After Jake explained where he thought he was, they determined he was still a good twenty minutes from Jordon's property. Chris then suggested where Jake park once he arrived, and Jake agreed

They both knew their next decision could be the one they'd live to regret. Jake brought it up first.

"So do they go forward without me or do we ask them to wait?" Both of them knew how critical those 5 minutes could be.

Chris didn't respond.

"How good are the guys from Kern?" Jake asked.

"Good in general, but in this case, well, these guys are working Sunday, day patrol, which means they are lowest on the totem pole - probably recent recruits."

Jake and Chris had previously agreed upon their roles: Chris was supposed to handle *intel*. Jake knew what he wanted Chris to say next.

For a long moment there was silence.

"Jake," Chris continued, "I'm going to go ahead and tell them where to park and ask them to wait for you, but if something gives them cause to move, they're going to have to go. Are you okay with that?"

Jake blew out the breath he was holding. "Yeah, and thanks."

"I didn't make that call for you," Chris insisted, "I made it for Jordon. I did what I thought was best for her. And no matter how this goes down, I want you to remember I handled intel, not you."

Jake now realized Chris also thought they were going to be too late.

***

What a sweetheart Greg is, Jordon thought, as she noticed the tools in the back of the truck; he called the tree trimmer after all. Jordon went out on to the porch, put the barking dogs inside, silently waived at the trimmer and then pointed to where he should park.

It appeared to Jordon as if he misunderstood her and pulled into a partially hidden area just under the trees.

After he parked, he got out of his truck and walked along the side of the house. When he passed the screen door. Jordon heard the dogs' growl; she was glad she left them inside.

***

Well, Ming thought, Alex was right about what she heard in court. It is dark here, and these trees sure as hell are overgrown. Now this bitch is bound to believe I was sent by County Fire.

As Ming approached the log porch, Jordon put her hand over the mouthpiece of the phone and whispered, "Thanks for coming. I've got to take this call. Just do what you need to do. I'll be with you in a few minutes."

"That's fine Miss, but I'm gonna need some help. Someone home, 'sides you, who can help?"

"No," she continued to whisper.

"Well, anyone else around?"

She shook her head no. "I'm it, but I'm all yours in a couple of minutes. Just do whatever you need to do and if you need a ladder or anything else, all my husband's tools are under the house; the door is open, its just around to your left."

Ming barely listened to anything she had to say beyond the words, 'I'm all yours.' And, he thought, the bitch never even asked who sent me.

***

Jordon went back inside the house to calm her dogs down. Sitting on her bed, petting the pups, Jordon's conversation with Diana was finally winding down. It seemed to Jordon, that Diana was now willing to cooperate, though just barely; at least she promised to meet with an alcohol counselor. If, Jordon concluded, Diana did that, and ultimately agreed she was an alcoholic, then Jordon could probably bring in an expert witness who would testify Diana couldn't remember any part of the rape because she was experiencing an alcoholic black out. Further, this expert could also explain to the jury that as a result of Diana being in denial about her alcoholism, she'd be in no position to disagree with any incorrect assumption Dr. Sandy Davidson would have made.

After a few more encouraging words, Jordon hung up the phone. Jordon was exhausted, yet she pounded on her bed with both fists. "To hell with you Mr. Ross," she yelled, "they'll be no plea bargain!"

Between my victim, Jordon thought, and my expert, the jury is going to understand exactly what happened that night, and then Ross, and his rapist client, will go down.

All at once, Jordon remembered the waiting tree-trimmer and darted toward the side door. A moment later her dogs bound off the bed and followed closely behind.

***

Unbeknownst to Jordon, between her pounding on the bed and the dog's haste to follow, the infamous long phone cord unraveled once again, this time leaving the receiver dangling in the air.

***

To keep the barking dogs at bay, Jordon closed the door behind her.

34

Sunday, April 5, 2006 2:12 p.m.

Reasonable Suspicion – Quantum of knowledge sufficient to induce an ordinary and cautious officer to believe criminal activity is at hand.

As soon as Diana put down the phone, it rang again. The caller was her receptionist; she told Diana she had a visitor named Arty. Diana didn't think she knew an Arty, but she came out to greet him nonetheless.

When Diana entered the lobby she didn't recognize anyone. A skinny man with stringy, black hair walked over to her. He stood too close while he softly stated that his name was Arty, and he was a bartender at Harvey's. He had, he said, photos of her in his car; photos taken the night she *partied* in I.V. He offered to bring them in. Diana suggested they go out to his car.

Diana still felt rattled by her conversation with Jordon and wasn't sure about much, but she knew she never wanted any photos taken of her in I.V. that night, to ever find their way into her TV studio.

***

Muratoto watched as Arty entered the TV studio and came out a few minutes later with Diana.

Diana looked uncomfortable, but willingly went inside Arty's car.

Without "reasonable suspicion," Muratoto knew he couldn't detain Arty. He decided instead to watch closely, be ready to follow them, and ask Jeff to call the S.F.P.D. for assistance.

***

Diana began to cry as she looked at the pictures and listened to Arty's threats about exposing her if she testified.

"But," she said though her tears, "this is proof he raped me. Where did you get these pictures?"

"I took them." Arty admitted. "But it doesn't look like rape to me; it looks like you were in the throes of ecstasy."

Diana began to panic. "No, no it doesn't." In truth, Diana wasn't sure how it looked, and she still couldn't remember how she acted.

"Looks to me," Arty offered, "like you are in a state of rapture. Arty's voice became soft and low. He put his hand on Diana's knee. "I, I saw you that night," he began, "at Harvey's. I noticed you right away. I thought you were beautiful and when I heard you were going to party on Del Playa in I.V. I called my buddy Cantera. Cantera tracked you down, it wasn't hard to find you... you are so beautiful." Arty put his hand on Diana's thigh. Diana felt frozen and trapped. "After Ernesto found you he called me. You were very fucked up by then. You wanted it." Arty started caressing Diana's shoulder. "So we thought Ernesto would fuck you and I'd take pictures." Arty showed her a photograph with Ernesto between Diana's legs; Diana thought she appeared unconscious. "Beautiful," Arty said, "no?"

35

Sunday, April 5, 2006 2:00 p.m.

Homicide – The killing of one human being by another.

Ming brought along all the tools he needed to do exactly what he'd intended to do. Still, he gathered some more from under Jordon's house; he wanted to keep up the façade for as long as he needed to.

"Okay," Jordon said as she stepped back outside, "so how'd you know someone would be home this weekend? We were all supposed to be sailing. Did my husband call you after I left?"

This bitch, Ming thought, is making this whole thing too easy, no need to even bullshit her about the fire department. "Yes, Ma'am" he answered, "that's what happened."

***

"What a Saint Greg is for remembering to call you."

Jordon then wondered if something was wrong; she thought she caught a glimpse of surprise in the tree trimmer's eyes. "I'm just shocked Greg thought I could help."

"Oh, ma'am he no tell me he thought you'd help. I thought I'd bring my helper, but he no come, and I know you here, and your husband, he make it sound important, and your tree she does look full, but, I *could* come back."

Jordon thought about it, but only for a moment. She wanted the tree trimmed, and she could use the break. Still, something felt wrong.

Ultimately, she rationalized, there was nothing suspicious about the gardener, and she was just being paranoid. Before she became a D.A. she was fearless, now that she knew about some of the danger that lurked out there, she'd become mistrustful. Jordon reminded herself she was in her mountain community and decided to turn off her paranoia and help. "No, no," she said, "let's do it!"

First, Ming explained he'd tie a rope around her. Then, he'd grab the other end, take it up the tree and tie the rope on a limb. After that, he'd saw the branch and with the weight of her body, she could direct where the limb should fall.

Jordon thought the trimmer's plan made sense. She didn't want the limb to hit her deck, house, or car. But, she also didn't want this stranger to tie her up. Still, she was sure that if Greg chose him, he had to be highly regarded. Even so, people with good reputations have been known to commit bad crimes. Jordon decided she'd let him put the rope around her waist but she'd keep both arms completely free.

Ming gave the rope around Jordon an extra tug. Then he climbed up the tree, and out of her view.

Moments later she heard a cracking sound.

"Damn," he yelled out. "This limb, she crack. I need 'nother tool. You hold still. If tree tear here, she could be hurt."

Jordon wasn't thrilled with the idea of standing still and anchoring the branch, but she wasn't really concerned; that is until her dogs started snarling.

***

Jake drove faster. He couldn't lose her, not now, not ever. Her safety meant everything to him. He arrived at the spot chosen by Chris just as the dust from the arrival of the other officers was beginning to clear. As soon as he got out of his car, he was approached by a member of the Kern County Sheriff's Department. "Agent Manchester, I'm Sergeant Larson I've been on the phone with Officer Valentine. He's talked to S.B.P.D. and S.B.F.D. they told him all about you. Listen, we're officially in charge, but you tell me: how do you want to proceed?"

Jake was glad they were willing to break protocol and listen to his input, but he wanted to be fully in charge.

"How many of you here?" Jake asked.

"Six officers, three cars, four of us are SWAT."

"I used to be a SWAT Team Leader, okay if I step in?"

Larson paused for a moment. "It's yours until I say so."

Jake quickly organized his thoughts as well as his new team. The silence coming from the direction of Jordon's cabin both comforted and terrified him.

Jake called Chris one last time before beginning his approach. "When," Jake now whispered, "was the last time you tried to call her?"

"Within the last forty five seconds. Jake there's been a change; the line's ringing busy, maybe it's just off the hook. Jake…" Jake could hear Chris' voice crack, "Jake, go get her."

Jake ran as quickly and as quietly as he could. He tried to watch out for sticks, but all he saw was an image of Jordon. The image was horrible, he was sure it was real: Jordon was covered with blood.

***

Ming climbed down the tree, ran around to the side of the house and then slowly, silently, walked toward her back.

The dogs continued to growl and snarl. Ming paused and decided to silence them. He walked towards the screen door. Brutus leaped up at him causing a small tear in the screen. Ming stepped back. No time to waste, he thought. Time for me to stab in the back, the bitch who stabbed my friends in the back. This, Ming declared, is justice.

***

Jake had each officer begin their final approach from a different area. Each of them was armed and trying to remain cognizant of their own, as well as each other's, physical bearings. From a short distance away, Jake heard the dogs and could see Ming grab Jordon. At the same moment Jake witnessed Deputy Bryne stumble out of the woods. All four of them looked shocked.

"Ming," Deputy Bryne commanded, "let go of Mrs. Danner and step back, now."

"Ming?" Jordon cried out.

"Deputy," Jake yelled, "don't move."

They all froze.

***

Ming put his hand across Jordon's shoulder and a knife up against her throat.

"Take one step closer to me, Pig," Ming commanded, "and I'll slit her throat." With one stroke Ming cut the rope off her waist, then he returned the knife to her throat, and started walking her backward toward his truck.

***

Jordon tried to keep her balance; she knew if she tripped, she'd die.

Suddenly, the dogs tore through the screen on the door. Jordon pushed Ming's arm away from her throat.

***

Jake fired.

The bullet shot through Ming's wrist and landed squarely in his gut. Ming's blood spattered all over Jordon's face and torso. The knife fell to the ground with a part of Ming's right hand still attached. Ming hung on to Jordon with his left hand until his strength gave out, then he slid down her body and on to the ground.

Jordon was now covered with Ming's blood; she stood perfectly still. Jake ran toward her while the other officers ran toward Ming. Jake took Jordon into his arms. Jordon's blood-soaked body clung to his.

Jake took hold of her shoulders and pushed her away. "Are you hit anywhere?"

Jordon just stared at him.

"JoJo, sweetheart, you have to answer me. Are you hurt?"

"Hurt?" Jordon was starting to respond. "No... I don't...I don't think so."

***

At first Jordon was confused, and started running her hands over her arms, and body. "I...I think, I think ..." Suddenly she was sinking down toward the ground.

***

Jake was right there to break her fall. He searched her body for wounds of any kind. It was the first time he really touched her, yet it felt so natural. Moments later, he was confident she'd escaped injury.

Shooting at Ming's moving hand, with an eye toward landing the bullet in his body, was the precision shot of Jake's career; the one he'd spent his life training for.

***

Jordon woke up between Jake's legs; the back of her head resting against his chest. She felt disoriented, safe, panicked, and comforted all at once. Jordon didn't know what she'd just said but Jake was carefully wiping off her mouth and telling her, "Never mind *that*, drink this." Jordon squinted and saw he was holding a cup of something to her lips; she smelled it first.

"...fine wine," she mumbled with her eyes still mostly closed, "...cheap stuff always gives me a head-ache..."

"That's my girl! Its water Jordon – drink it. Well, Gentlemen I think it's fair to say, D.A. Danner is back. Jordon, open your eyes and meet your rescuers."

Squinting Jordon looked around and saw four uniformed men staring at her. Two more men were standing a little ways off; one was on a telephone and the other was standing by the tree trimmer's lifeless body. Before Jordon could say a word the officer on the phone yelled, "How many ambulances?"

"JoJo," Jake whispered softly, "do you need an ambulance?"

Jordon turned slowly and faced him. "I don't think so, I think I just felt a little lightheaded and then the next thing I knew I was in your arms."

"Yeah," Jake said still whispering, but now smiling, "I've been known to have that effect on women."

Jordon hit his arm; what water remained in the cup splashed on her face. She put her hands up to her face and felt something. As she took her, now bloody, hands away she screamed, "Oh my God!"

"Take it easy Champ," Jake offered "That's not your blood, but when you are feeling up to it we do need to get you cleaned up."

Jordon felt queasy all over again. "Not my blood?"

"No, that's his blood," Jake slowly answered. "Jordon, he's dead, and as soon as you can stand up, we need to get you in the shower. Meanwhile, no more opening your mouth until then."

Jake slowly helped her up. Once she was standing, she felt weak again and put her head on his chest.

"How 'bout I just stay here?" Jordon asked as she nuzzled into his neck.

"No," he whispered, "that's just not safe."

You're telling me, she thought, as she started to once again fade away.

***

Jake had never known such joy. He had saved the life of the woman he loved and now she was safely snuggling up against him. He wanted her to stay there forever, but first she had to take a shower. He didn't want any of that bastard's blood to find its way into her body. "Okay JoJo pay attention." He thought she was still in shock. "You've rested long enough. I'm taking you into the shower."

***

Jordon was starting to become and stay oriented "Yeah," she whispered, now trying to bring humor in to a situation that completely baffled her, "first you try to give me cheap wine then you try to get me into a shower." The humor wasn't working, Jordon was still terrified. "Jake what's going on?"

"Jordon, stop talking. First we need to get you cleaned up, and then I'll tell you everything. That man's blood could be as dangerous as the knife."

Jake began to walk her toward the house.

Once inside the bedroom he asked if she wanted him to undress her.

As tempting as that would have been at any other moment, Jordon didn't want that now. The first time she appeared naked in front of Jake, she wanted to feel in control. Now she felt anything but in control; she felt vulnerable, shaky, and a little bit spiritual.

***

Jake waited in Jordon's bedroom until she went into the bathroom. Once he heard the water running he asked another officer to stand by while he ran out to the Paradise van, grabbed his real clothes, and changed out of his blood-caked, gardener's overalls. Next, he called Paul Howe.

Jake assured Paul Jordon was fine, and then Jake heard more details about Riverstone's confession. Howe sounded gleeful and was particularly jubilant when he described Riverstone's face as he was being taken into custody.

***

When Jordon came out of the shower she appeared perfectly clean, uninjured, and completely enveloped in a thick white terry cloth robe. Jake thought she had never looked more beautiful.

***

Once they sat down on her bed Jake told her all about the Ming-Riverstone connection. Jordon was too tired to ask too many questions, but she now clearly understood Ming and Riverstone had conspired to kill her.

"But how did they know where I was or what their plan would be?"

"Apparently," Jake answered, "somehow Alexandra got word to Ming about what she overheard you say to the courtroom clerk. Did you say something about going up to your mountain home, alone, this weekend?"

Jordon nodded.

"I guess Alexandra also heard you complain about how overgrown the trees were. I assume Ming and River-stone cooked up their plan up after that, and, apparently as careful as you are about not listing your Santa Barbara address, references to, or pictures of, your Mt. Able home appears in a few of your write-ups; write-ups Riverstone confessed to finding on the internet."

Jordon was now beginning to understand she'd been moments away from being murdered. She was about to ask a follow up question, when there was a knock at her bedroom door.

Sergeant Larson entered the room. He wanted them to know the coroner called and said he wouldn't be there for hours. Larson didn't want Jordon to have to remain at her home with the corpse, so he said they could leave as soon as they gave their statements to the deputies.

Jordon said she was ready to give her statement right away, and Jake concurred.

***

Hours later, Jake and Jordon were finally free to leave. As they walked out of the living room, they were told that one of the Santa Barbara deputies had offered to take back Jordon's car, dogs, and file boxes.

Jordon felt appreciative and relieved; at the moment she couldn't imagine driving or caring for her pups. Once she was inside Jake's van, she took one last look through the back window. Her beautiful log home had metamorphosed into a Hollywood set, complete with cameras, CSI agents, people with walkie-talkies, and even a news helicopter hovering just overhead.

Jordon's precious hideaway was gone forever, but she had survived.

***

In case there was ever any doubt in Jake's mind, he was now sure how much she truly meant to him. Fearing he'd be too late to save her was the worst moment of his life, and saving her was the best. He now knew he could never let her go.

***

Jordon looked over at Jake - he'd become her hero; he'd saved her life. She now not only wanted to spend the rest of her life with him, she also felt she owed him at least that much. Maybe he could get a transfer to L.A. She would stay in Santa Barbara until Sam left for college and Greg...

Jake broke their silence. "I know we have a lot to talk about, but how 'bout we call Chris first. I know he'd love to hear your voice. Sounds like Chris is another fan of yours, and he did a great job organizing your rescue. After that, we can grab some food and talk. You don't look like you've had a real meal for days and I'm suddenly starving." Jake handed Jordon his phone.

Jordon looked at her watch. She knew her family wouldn't be back for hours and she agreed they had to eat and talk; probably in that order.

"I know a perfect restaurant," she said, "it will still be open, and it's on our way home. It looks out over the Santa Paula Airport; they specialize in burgers and even have decent bourbon."

"Sounds ideal," Jake said, as he reached over and put his hand on her knee. In response, she cuddled closer to him and temporarily rested her head on his shoulder. A moment later, she sighed and dialed. Chris answered right away.

"So, you saved her, eh?"

"No, I *am* her."

"Jordon Danner, your voice never sounded sweeter. How the hell are you?"

"Good. Actually, great, and I hear you're the reason I'm still among the living."

"Bullshit, I just helped. Jake Manchester's your man."

So it seems, she thought.

After Jordon and Chris spoke for a few more minutes Jordon put Chris on speaker-phone. After a few, "You're the man," "No, you're the man," comments between the two, Jake and Chris agreed to meet for a beer sometime in the near future.

After Jake put his phone away, Jordon returned to her position on his shoulder and fell asleep.

***

Jordon woke up when Jake pulled on the emergency break in the parking lot of Langdon's Airport Restaurant.

"Is this the place?" he asked.

Jordon briefly looked around. "Yep."

When they stepped out of the car they smelled grilled onions and burgers. "Damn," Jake offered, "*that* smells good!"

It was now close to 9 o'clock: the restaurant was almost empty and half closed. Jordon asked for a booth by the window, because she wanted them to be able to see the night stars and the lights from the incoming planes.

36

Sunday, April 5, 2006 2:15 p.m.

Probable Cause - Quantum of knowledge sufficient to cause the average reasonable person to believe a crime has been committed by a particular suspect. When a law enforcement officer feels the standard of probable cause has been reached, s/he can affect an arrest.

Muratoto and his partner Jeff stood by until Muratoto could see Arty put his hand on to Diana's shoulder. "Enough", he said. They walked over to the driver's side. Muratoto pulled open the door and ordered Arty out. Jeff took Arty into custody.

Diana screamed and drew her knees up to her chest. Muratoto showed her his badge, reminded her they'd met before, and promised her she was now safe. Eventually, she came out of the car and together they walked back into her office. Once there, they called her parents who said they'd be over right away.

While they waited for her parents, Muratoto listened as Diana told him what happened in the car and about her recent conversation with Jordon. Soon Muratoto acknowledged he was an alcoholic who'd been sober for twelve years. Muratoto's admission seemed to comfort, and perhaps encourage Diana. Within a half hour, Diana's parents picked her up and Muratoto returned to his car to talk to Arty, who fully admitted his involvement. Essentially, he told Muratoto the same thing he'd told Diana, only he described Diana as, "merely a photo–op."

Muratoto then booked Arty into a San Francisco jail.

Once Arty was in custody Muratoto tried to call Jordon at her mountain house, but no one answered. He then decided to call her office the next morning.

37

Sunday, April 5, 2006 9:30 p.m.

Joint Resolution – A resolution passed by both parties subject to executive veto.

Jake loved the restaurant from the moment they walked in. It looked like it had been built in the 50's and neither it, nor the people inside, seemed to have changed much since then.

Jordon and Jake were escorted to a blue, over-sized Naugahyde booth. The bench seating was both worn and lumpy. After shifting slightly, Jake melted right in.

Knowing if he had an "Old Fashion" now he'd be sober by the time he drove again, and considering what they were about to discuss, Jake ordered a double for himself and a single for Jordon.

***

When the waitress walked away, they looked into each other's eyes. For a moment, they were the only two people who existed. Once that moment passed, they were back in purgatory, caught somewhere between great pleasure and even greater pain.

Fearful of the decision they had to make, and recognizing the grief that was sure to follow, they both turned and stared at the runway lights.

***

Jordon left her hand on the table, hoping Jake would take it, and he did.

"I can't believe I almost lost you." He exhaled deeply; tears filled his eyes.

When Jordon turned to face him, she too was crying. "I can't believe you saved my life." Jordon put her other hand on top of his.

"I didn't do it alone; you and the dogs made it possible."

Jordon smiled.

The waitress arrived with their drinks. He let go. Jordon put her hands in her lap and glanced up at their waitress. Her pin bore the name Evelyn. Evelyn had hard hair, and soft eyes. Evelyn glanced at each of them; her experienced look conveyed much. Jordon thought Evelyn must have seen lovers in pain too many times: she clearly doesn't know what's going on with us, but she seems to be aching for us just the same.

"I'll come back in a few minutes," Evelyn offered. "You two just take your time."

If only we could, Jordon thought.

***

Jake and Jordon nodded. Jordon looked out the window as Jake watched over her; Jake was worried. He knew all about the stages of shock and wanted to be there for her during each one of them. He now understood why some believed if you saved a life they were your responsibility forever. If only…

"So, what are you thinking about?" Jordon asked.

He took her nearby hand again. "The day, the events, the emotions. I guess I'm just letting it all sink in slowly. How're you doing?"

"I think I'm still in shock. I'm sort of in this twilight zone. There's so much to think about - where we've been, where we are, where we're going."

"How 'bout we start with where we're going, but I suggest we order, eat, and talk on a full stomach."

Jake motioned for Evelyn, while Jordon looked at the window.

Jake wanted to delay his talk with Jordon for just a few minutes longer; the thought of potentially losing her again terrified him.

***

Jordon's world had spun out of control. She turned, focused on the parked aircraft, and wondered what their owner's lives were like.

By the time Jordon faced Jake again, she realized he was already ordering her dinner.

As soon as their waitress walked away Jake smiled. "Awfully ballsy of me to order for you and not even make it your usual rabbit food, but you've got to eat something with substance, especially after you've downed that drink. I make it a practice of never taking advantage of drunk women, especially when they are in shock, having just almost been killed."

"You make a practice of it? So you've done this be-fore?"

"Oh, yes, countless times."

They both smiled, but not for long; their bread had arrived. They knew that life altering decisions had to be made, this night, at this table, but for now there were two steaming warm rolls to be eaten. Jake ate his quickly, while Jordon buttered hers slowly, tore it in half, and shared it with him. Jake smiled again and devoured it.

***

Jake was sure the roll she buttered tasted better than the previous one. After savoring his last swallow of Jack Daniels, he decided to start with the easy stuff. "So are you all squared away on the cases?"

"Yep, remarkably so. I just need to figure out if I can get the shrink's letter into evidence. Even if I can't, with all the extra evidence you found, I'm thinking West will probably plead."

"Plead? How do you figure that?"

"Well, based upon West's pattern and practice of choosing elderly victims, I think I can now also charge Ruthie's murder as a hate crime, the "protected class" being the elderly; in which case, I think we should reconsider the death penalty. The way I figure it, once the defense sorts out what you discovered, they'll come to me and offer to plead guilty if we just stick with life without possibility of parole."

Jordon paused and took a deep breath. "And, with a plea they'd also give up their right to appeal–"

"And," Jake asked, "that's it, right?" Jake knew he couldn't hide how unsettled that thought made him feel.

"As far as that case goes," Jordon answered. "But, then there's the murder charge in Kansas and the conspiracy charge against Riverstone. I'm not sure what Paul and the Attorney General's office will do with that son-of-a-bitch, but it seems to me he gave you very little." Jordon could hear herself getting upset and beginning to ramble. "I really don't think, had it been me, that I would have given him any kind of immunity."

Jake felt defensive. "Jordon, you've got to be kidding. Someone's life was at stake. At first I had no idea it was yours, and that's when we offered him use immunity, but once I found out it was you, I would have given him anything." Jake was beginning to get angry. "And if the situation presented itself again, I'd do the same damn thing."

Jake turned away and looked toward the oncoming waitress. He did feel somewhat guilty. At the time, he knew he and Paul probably didn't have the authority to offer Riverstone immunity, but at the time, Jake wasn't thinking about jurisdiction and laws, he was thinking about saving someone's life.

***

Jordon reached across the table and put her hand on the side of his flushed face. "I'm sorry. You are, and were, right. Sometimes the D.A. in me pushes the human being aside." Jordon smiled and then looked up. Their medium rare burgers teeming with grilled onions arrived. Jordon reluctantly took away her hand. "Good choice Jake-o, this smells great!"

They both laughed at her use of the name Jake-o, she'd never called him that before. Without further discussion he handed her the mustard, while she passed him the ketchup. It was yet another subtle, but meaningful, testament to how well they knew each other, and how much they cared.

***

Jake thought the burger was the best he'd ever eaten and was considering ordering another one, when Jordon's cell phone rang.

They looked at her phone to see who was calling. The space for the number only indicated, "BLOCKED."

"Hello?"

Within a matter of seconds, Jake could tell something horrible had happened. Jordon was pale. She looked up at him, fear glossing her eyes. Jordon kept asking, "Is he alright? Are you sure he's alright?" She seemed somewhat relieved by whatever she was hearing until she asked, "A cutter? Why aren't you sending a helicopter?" But, a helicopter would get there faster." "What do you mean you don't have one that…that's got to be bullshit I'll pay for it!"

Jordon stopped arguing, and started listening, as well as crying. Moments later she murmured, "Call me as soon as you know anything."

As soon as she hung up she told Jake everything she'd learned. She sounded precise. He knew sounding that way sometimes made her feel in control, but now she looked like she felt: completely out of control.

Jake knew not to touch her at that moment, so he sat as far forward as he could and sent her, through his eyes, all the support he dared.

Struggling with every word and image, she explained that the call was from the Coast Guard. "…Sam finally caught a calico bass, he was very excited. He also found an old piece of glass - a broken bottle actually - something he knew Greg would like. Anyway, as soon as Sam came back to the boat George started yelling for him to pull up the anchor. Sam threw his gear off, put his spear on a ledge and ran to help. But, in all the excitement he forgot he'd tucked that piece of glass in his vest. And while Sam was pulling up the anchor his finger got caught up against something, something called a winch, and it really hurt."

Jordon's tears made it almost impossible for her to continue. She paused, took a deep-quivering breath, and went on. "So Sam screamed for Greg and Greg came running. On his way to save Sam, Greg stepped on Sam's vest. The big piece of ragged glass tore way into the bottom of Greg's foot. Greg pulled the chunk of glass out, but lost his footing and bumped into the spear. The spear's blade went through Greg's jeans, slicing into his calf. Greg was badly cut, but he kept running to help Sam. As soon as Greg got to Sam, Greg pulled hard on the rope and Sam's hand was free. Then Greg pulled up the anchor and immediately tended to Sam's hand. Meanwhile blood must have been coming out of Greg's foot and calf, but he didn't tell either of the boys… Greg was bleeding out, and all he cared about were his kids."

Jordon began crying harder. Jake didn't dare speak.

"Once Sam was taken care of, Greg started to go into shock. Moments later *my husband* passed out." By now, Jordon was crying hysterically and everyone in the restaurant was staring.

"Jordon," Jake asked, "is Greg still alive?"

"Barely."

"Is the Coast Guard on their way?"

"Yes, but only by some damn cutter boat. They don't have the right kind of helicopter nearby."

"What about Sam?"

"He's okay, just shaken up. But I'm sure he's busy blaming himself for everything." Her sobs became louder. "And now he probably thinks his father's going to die and it's all his fault, and all he was trying to do was to bring his dad a buried treasure and me a Bass. Oh, my poor baby. And poor George is probably sick with worry and I'm sitting here…"

She looked devastated. Jake stood up.

"Where are you going?"

"To find Greg a helicopter."

"What? Where?"

As soon as Jake walked away from the table he was speaking on his cell phone.

Jordon considered calling their other sons, Anthony and Ray, but wasn't sure if she should worry them. A moment later, she knew she had to, they'd always been that kind of family - they never went though tough times alone.

Jordon reached Anthony first. He'd just returned from his weekend in San Diego. Although he sounded upbeat when he answered, as soon as he heard her voice he just listened.

After she told him what happened, Jordon knew they wanted to reassure each other, but words failed them both. When Jordon saw Jake walk back in, she said she had to go.

"Mom," Anthony asked, "do you think Dad's gonna die?"

"Sweetheart, I don't know, but I'll call you as soon as I know *anything*."

"And I'll call Ray now. You just do what you gotta do to save Dad."

They ended the call with their usual proclamations of love, but this time, there was unrestrained sadness in each of their voices.

Jordon looked toward Jake. He answered her unspoken question. "There's an emergency navy helicopter parked here. A navy pilot and doctor are on their way. You will be taking off in about 12 minutes."

"But how..? I'll be taking off?"

"Yes, I assumed you'd want to go."

She looked into his eyes. "You assumed right."

"You love him."

"How do you know?"

"Because I watched your face when you began to imagine he might be dead. It was my face a few hours ago. It was a face without life. You may think you're in love with me, but he's still your life."

Jordon couldn't disagree, though she could tell Jake was still hoping she would.

"What about us?" she asked. Her eyes were pleading with him to find a way for them not to say good-bye.

Instead he said, "Let's go out to the office, they'll be here any minute."

Jake put out his hand; Jordon took it.

They walked across the parking lot clutching each other's hands. Jordon had so much to say but knew none of it would change what was about to happen.

When they got to the airport office they noted a small sign, **CP Aviation**, but the door was locked. The air was cold. The day's events, along with what was about to occur, suddenly caught up with her. She steadied her shaking body by placing her hand on the door. Jake put his back up against the office's cold brick wall and gathered her up in his arms.

Her back was against his chest - just the way it had been a few hours ago. He exhaled; the air sent a chill down her spine.

"You're right you know," she whispered.

***

He was still hoping he wasn't.

"You and I have had these feelings for a long time," she continued, "and the single reason I could never act on them was Greg, and my commitment to our family. Still, I feel so torn, not just between the two of you, but my heart feels torn - really ripped in two.   Jake, I will always miss you."

Jake couldn't respond; he just held her closer.

"Should I call you once we get back?" she asked, knowing he'd say 'no.'

"No," he answered, "I'll know what's going on and if you need me, I'll find you. I think I'm going to need some time to shift gears." In spite of his effort not to, Jake held her even closer.

"Jake, I'm so sorry. I should never have let us get this close."

Jake shook his head. "Getting close to you has been one of the single greatest experiences of my life. You're remarkable in everyway. You've raised the bar about what I think a woman can be and I'm sure someday I'll find someone." He wasn't sure at all, and at that moment he never wanted Jordon to leave his arms.

"District Attorney Danner?" A voice came out of the darkness.

Two military looking men approached. "And you must be Agent Manchester."

"Yes, I am. Thank you for coming. Do you have everything you need?"

The other military man stepped forward. "I'm Doctor Roberts. I understand we're talking about a bleeding stab wound or two. I've got everything I need with me or it's on board. Sergeant Wilkins knows where we're headed so I think we're ready to go. District Attorney Danner, are you all set?"

Jordon hadn't spoken yet. "Yes," she eked out, "and thank you."

Sergeant Wilkins led the way and entered the helicopter first. He was followed by Doctor Roberts.

The blades began to whirl. Jake took her in his arms. There were no more words, they hugged one last time, and then she went up the steps.

Jordon collapsed into her seat and was thankful for both the darkness and the noise.

38

Monday, April 6, 2006 8:30 a.m.

Justice – That state of being where the finality is in accord with the initial insult

"Rick Cohn for the People. I assume the Court is aware of all The Danners have been through."

"Yes," Judge Ames replied. "I heard about it on the news this morning. How are they?"

"I was just at the hospital before I came here. D.A. Danner is unharmed. Mr. Danner is out of the Intensive Care Unit and smiling. He's got his wife and their four sons right there with him, so I'm sure a full recovery is imminent." Rick smiled. It had been a long night. Rick was there with Anthony and Ray when the helicopter arrived on the hospital's roof.

"That's good to hear, please give them all our best wishes. Now, how would you like to proceed today?"

Philip Adler stood up. "Your Honor, I spoke with Agent Manchester this morning. There were an uncanny number of new developments that occurred this weekend. Assuming everything he has communicated is correct, and I have no reason to disbelieve him, I expect my client will plead guilty as charged. We just need about a month to review the new discovery and communicate with another prosecutor in Kansas."

"Kansas?" Judge Ames looked baffled, but everyone knew the lawyers couldn't give him any further information until they reached a deal. "Sounds like it's been quite a weekend all around. Alright then, I'll see you all back here on May 6th." Judge Ames rose to leave the bench.

"Your Honor, I'm Ted Ross, attorney for Mr. Cantera. I was to talk to Ms. Danner this morning. I had conveyed an offer to her on our case which I said would expire this morning, but under these circumstances–"

"The offer," Rick Cohn interrupted, "is rejected." Rick turned and walked toward the courtroom door.

"Anything else Mr. Ross?" Judge Ames asked.

"Ah," Ted looked around, "I guess not, thank you."

Ted left in a hurry and caught up to Rick in the hall-way.

"Mr. Cohn," Ted called, as he ran after Rick. "I'm so sorry to hear about Ms. Danner."

Rick stopped but didn't respond. He knew all about Ross' reputation for being both disingenuous and manipulative.

Ted Ross continued, "I hate for her to go to trial in a month's time after all she's been through. I just feel so bad for her and..."

Rick put up his hand. "Save your sympathy for your client, Mr. Ross, he'll need it after she kicks your ass. And by the way, I think you might want to call Detective Muratoto he has some new 'discovery' for you."

Tedd Ross froze. Rick kept walking.

***

"You didn't really tell him I'd kick his ass, did you?" Jordon asked.

"Of course I did." Rick answered smiling broadly.

"Why?" Jordon was starting to smile.

"Because it's true, you will kick his ass. Because in a month's time your victim will walk into that courtroom with her head held high. Beyond that, it sounds like young Arty's going to give you all the corroborating testimony and photos you could hope for."

Jordon's smile didn't fade. "So, Muratoto called you this morning after he had already left me a five minute voicemail message?"

"Yep, and he is very pumped up. Apparently he thinks he has convinced Arty that the best thing he can do is come clean and testify for the prosecution."

"Well, I'm not quite as optimistic as you and Muratoto are, but I did talk to Diana a little while ago. She is doing remarkably well. It seems talking to Muratoto and seeing the photos, as terrifying as they were, actually helped her with some unanswered fears and questions. I also think having her parents arrive so soon after Arty was arrested, will help support her sobriety."

Jordon exhaled, she was exhausted. She needed to rest and focus on Greg.

"Well, it's been one hell of a weekend," she said. "Rick, I love you, but you've got to go. All this talk about the office is not helping my husband heal. I'll walk you out to the elevator."

"Greg, old man, I'm sorry." Rick smiled. "It appears I have overstayed my welcome."

Greg smiled in return. "Don't listen to her, it's always great to see you, but I do think I'm about ready for a nap. Please come by later if you feel like it. I'll probably go to sleep early, and I'm sure Jordon would love to talk to you some more."

***

Rick reached over and squeezed Greg's shoulder. "Wild horses, or tenacious prosecutors, couldn't keep me away." Rick teared up, he was deeply appreciative that Jake secured the helicopter and Greg was safe. "Okay, Buddy," Rick added, "get some rest. And as our famous Governor used to say, 'I'll be back!'" Rick turned to leave and Jordon followed.

On the way to the elevator Rick asked, "So, have you heard from our hero?"

Jordon's sudden sadness was obvious. "No, have you?"

Rick nodded, "Yeah, he called me from the airport just before I got here. He wanted to know how things went in court and of course he wanted an update on you, and your family. I sure hope we get to work with him again."

Rick looked over at Jordon. She teared up, nodded slowly, and swallowed hard. Rick still wasn't sure just how close she and Jake had become, but Rick knew as close as he and Jordon were, he should never ask. Rick just shook his head and continued, "He's a heck of an A.T.F. agent."

Jordon nodded, smiled slightly and added, "Intoxicating."

Rick was sure if Jordon ever wanted to say more, she would. For now, she clearly wanted to focus on her family.

Rick and Jordon briefly hugged. Then Rick pushed the elevator button and they waited. Rick knew he'd be back in a few hours. He was sure Jordon needed him, and he wanted to spend as much time with her as he could. Rick had only heard about some of what occurred at Jordon's cabin, but he was painfully aware that he'd almost lost his best friend. "Have you told Greg about your near-death experience yet?

"Nope, I don't want to upset him. He's still too weak."

"Well, he's going to find out soon, either through someone else or the media. I think he should hear it from you."

"He will," she answered somewhat defensively, "all in good time."

The elevator arrived and Rick walked in. "Call if you need anything. I can be here for you in a flash."

Jordon smiled. "You always are."

39

Monday April 6, 3:10 p.m.

"Someday I'll wish upon a star and wake up where the clouds are far behind me…" Izzy

When Jordon walked back into the hospital room Greg was asleep. She pulled a chair over to his bedside, sat down, and ran her fingers though his hair.

Greg's eyelashes fluttered, but he kept his eyes shut. Jordon later assumed it was because he didn't want to see her face when he questioned her.

"I almost lost you didn't I?" he asked.

Jordon wasn't sure if he meant because he almost died, or because he found out about her experience, or because he sensed what she'd been feeling toward Jake. Regardless, the answer was the same.

"Yes," she said as she took his hand.

"But I didn't," he weakly asserted, "and that's all that matters." Tears began to seep from his closed eyes, pause on his lashes, and float down his cheeks.

"No, you didn't," Jordon said, first wiping his tears and then her own. "And if, or when, you're ready for more details," Jordon continued, "just ask." Jordon knew sometimes Greg preferred to remain in the dark.

Greg barely opened his red eyes. "Maybe I'll ask while we're on a beach walk, somewhere in…Hawaii?"

Jordon looked playfully shocked. "So, you heard huh? Well, did you know, as soon as your doctor clears you, we're finally going to take Jan up on her offer to lend us her condo in Maui? Hey, by the way, which one of our little twerps ruined my surprise?"

They both nodded and answered at the same time.

"Baby Sam!"

A second later, as if on cue, Sam walked in the hospital room followed by his more reverent older brothers. Sam was playing his ukulele and singing Izzy's Hawaiian version of "Somewhere over the Rainbow." All their sons entered wearing, hastily-purchased, Hawaiian shirts.

Anthony walked around to the other side of the bed and put his hand on his father's shoulder.

"Aloha!" Sam announced.

Sam was followed by Ray, who carried the loudest shirt of all. The shirt was covered with sunshine and Buddha's. "A shirt made for a hero and a king!" Ray exclaimed as he rhythmically swirled, and then laid the shirt over Greg's hospital gown.

Behind Ray, George stepped forward; still hiding a lei behind his back. "And flowers," George said placing the lei over Jordon's head, "for our queen mother." He then gently hugged her, and whispered, "Hey Bubba."

Jordon increased the intensity of their embrace; as she did, she carelessly crushed a few of the more delicate flowers, thereby releasing Awapuchi - another intoxicating agent. Jordon breathed in the aroma and the moment. Finally she whispered, "Home Now."

THE END

Epilogue

According to the Department of Justice, in 2004, 94,635 females, nationwide, were victims of reported forcible rapes. All reliable sources agree, the crime of rape, in general, is under-reported, and the crime of rape of an intoxicated person, is grossly under-reported. Authorities from college campus' across the country universally believe that well over 50% of their female students, who are raped, were intoxicated at the time of the assault.

When an intoxicated victim is raped they suffer long-lasting effects as a result of having their body, soul, and psyche, violated.

According to the Department of Homeland Security, U.S. Fire Administration, in 2004 there were approximately 36,500 arsons nationwide; cumulatively they resulted in 320 civilian deaths.

Arson is not a victimless crime.

According to the Bureau of Justice Statistics, in 2000, almost 121,000 seniors age 65 and over experienced a violent victimization. During that same year the Federal Bureau of Investigation reported 574 murders of elders.

When we fail to investigate and prosecute elder abuse we desecrate our past and future.

At first blush these violent crimes may appear less heinous then some, but only to those who haven't felt their impact.

Throughout the country Rape Crisis Advocates, Arson Investigation Teams, and Protective Service Workers remain, for the most part, underappreciated and underpaid; but they only remain unsung heroes until they are called into action.